Military Privilege
Book Two
Justice For All Series

BY
JL Redington

©JL Redington 2015

No part of this publication may be reproduced, or stored in a retrieval system, or transmitted in any form or by any means, electronic, mechanical, photocopying, recording or otherwise without written permission of the author.

Table of Contents

Chapter One
Chapter Two
Chapter Three
Chapter Four
Chapter Five
Chapter Six
Chapter Seven
Chapter Eight
Chapter Nine
Chapter Ten
Chapter Eleven
Chapter Twelve
Chapter Thirteen
Chapter Fourteen
Chapter Fifteen
Chapter Sixteen
Chapter Seventeen
Chapter Eighteen
Chapter Nineteen
Chapter Twenty
Chapter Twenty-One
Chapter Twenty-Two
Chapter Twenty-Three
Chapter Twenty-Four
Chapter Twenty-Five
Chapter Twenty-Six
Chapter Twenty-Seven
Chapter Twenty-Eight

Chapter Twenty-Nine
Eiplogue

Chapter One

It was early spring in and rain poured over D.C. The sky was dark, making the hour difficult to tell for certain. Was it late afternoon or early evening? Even the streetlights didn't know for sure and they shone through the rain, forcing murkiness down alleyways and in deep corners.

Tope Daniels slipped quietly from shadow to shadow, watching. Had he been followed? Had his cover really been blown? The only way to know for sure was to step out of the shadows and act normal.

This part of down was desolate slums with boarded up storefronts, completely abandoned by shoppers and the hustle of busy streets. Not the kind of place you shopped in, more like the kind of place you avoided. Rain pelted his jet-black hair, cascading down his forehead and into his placid blue eyes. He wasn't as tall as some of his friends at the agency, but at five feet eleven inches and slender, he could hide easier than the bigger guys. At least that's what he told himself.

Tope didn't think he'd been discovered, in spite of the information he'd been slipped only minutes ago. If he was, his superiors at the FBI were going to be doing a war dance, and he was going to be quite dead, neither of which was particularly good. He wouldn't ever work another undercover op because his picture would be distributed to all the mob families, and from there, to anyone else the mob families could think of. Undercover work for Tope wasn't going to happen if he'd been made.

They were deep into this operation and having gotten all the evidence they needed for the investigation of several mob extortion plots, the agency was about to swoop in for the arrests. Initially, Tope was to be arrested as part of those arrests to eliminate the possibility of being 'made' as the rat in the organization. However, after the threat of his discovery came to light, a change was made. It was decided he would discreetly disappear just prior to the raid by the agency, and that was what he was about to do. Disappear.

Three black FBI SUVs sped by, heading toward the home he'd been meeting in for the last year. No lights, no sirens. He recognized them as the cavalry, sent to do the arresting. It was time for him to step out of his hiding place and make sure he'd not been seen. He moved into the street and began walking as though he'd been around the block several times, not in a particular hurry.

A car came up behind him, creeping slowly, tires crunching on the soaked asphalt. He'd definitely been made; its slow approach was a dead giveaway. *Bad use of the term, for sure,* he thought to himself. Slipping smoothly into an alley to his right, he hid behind a pile of boards and pallets. Within seconds, he heard the bullets hit the wood. The organization had figured it out.

Drawing his weapon, he aimed and fired, hitting the passenger side of the car, missing the passenger who was firing at him, and hitting the driver. In reflex to the bullet, the driver hit the gas and the car careened out of control flying into an abandoned storefront and coming to an abrupt stop, its back end protruding from the broken glass, chunks of plywood and pieces of doorway. Tope peeked around the corner in time to see the passenger stagger from the car, blood running down the side of his head. The man looked up as Tope stepped from the alleyway. It was Masa, one of the bodyguards for the family the FBI had just successfully infiltrated. Masa stared at his prey for only a second before raising his gun. The gun shook as Masa clearly struggled to focus and keep his aim steady. Tope was lucky on this one. Masa was a perfect shot. Only the head wound could make his aim so erratic.

Tope smoothly lifted his gun with both hands and fired first, dropping the man to the pavement beside the car. All was quiet. An FBI SUV swerved to the curb and the passenger door flew open.

"Get in."

Tope didn't need a second invitation. He jumped into the backseat and slammed the door. The car sped from the scene with no one giving chase. The mess would be cleaned up, media questions answered, as much as protocol would allow, and the incident would be reported the next morning in the paper as an accident caused by a drunk driver. However, Tope was the problem now.

Someone in the organization had identified him as the rat. It was a near certainty that some of the perps would escape. Most of those would be caught and dealt with, others wouldn't, and Tope's face would be etched in their brains like claw marks on soft wood. There would be discussions about this in the days to come at the agency, and Tope was sure he'd go underground until they could figure out where to place him and what he'd do once he got there.

The operation seemed such a waste to him now. His uncle Jack was murdered in Iowa while Tope was deep undercover and he'd been unable to attend the funeral. He'd mourned in silence, knowing if he left the operation at that point, he'd have been made for sure. And yet, here he was. His cover was blown anyway. He should have gone to the funeral, for all the good it had done to stay.

As the SUV sped through the streets of D.C., Tope mentally flipped through pictures of his uncle and best friend. Only three years old when Tope was born, he and Jack were inseparable as they grew up. Jack was a 'second family' for his parents, born when his older sisters were teenagers - Kendalyn was 18, and Summer was 16. Kendalyn married when Jack was two years old and a year later she had Tope, making Tope's uncle only three years older than his nephew.

Kendalyn and her husband, Trent, met in Topeka when they were both in school. Because of that, the couple had a warm spot in their hearts for the city, and decided when their son was born, his name would be Tope. As Tope grew, it was clear he and Jack would not just be uncle and nephew, but the best of friends. When a job change necessitated a move by Jack's parents to the small mid-western town of Blakely, Iowa, Tope was flown out every summer to spend the days with his uncle. They had a good time teasing the locals about that. They'd looked so much alike that often people couldn't tell them apart. Tope smiled softly. The city continued to race by, blurred by speed and memories.

"I hope the silence back there is because you're planning your presentation to our most patient team leader." The driver, Tom Damons, chuckled as he glanced into the rearview mirror. "You're gonna need a good story for the boss on this one. I hope you're ready. That mess you left back there is going to take some creative clean up."

"There's not much to tell," replied Tope. "How did the raid go down? Did they get everyone?"

"No idea. I was told to go get you before I could get out of the car. Winston was concerned you'd been followed and told me to retrieve you. I figured you'd be where all the gunfire was coming from."

Special Agent Andre Winston was now Tope's immediate supervisor. Tall and a few years older than Tope, he was an imposing man with black hair and raven dark eyes. He'd worked with Max Menetti when he was the Assistant Criminal Investigative Director and now his son-in-law, Cayman Richards, who'd taken Max's place when he'd retired. Andre knew how things worked at the FBI. He was a good man, solid and trustworthy, and reported directly to the team leader, Patrick Richards, Cayman's brother.

With the betrayal the Bureau had endured, it was good to know the people who could be trusted. That betrayal, by one William Grantham, was behind them now, but the sting of it still burned in many agents. Grantham had killed one of his own agents in broad daylight and would have killed more if it suited his needs. Currently he was in prison and would stay there for the remainder of his life without the possibility of parole. That suited the Bureau just fine. Death by firing squad was too good for Grantham. He needed to rot in prison, knowing he'd never, ever, see freedom again.

"Yeah, that's usually where I am, but you know it's not my fault, right? It's where the bosses always put me, right in the line of fire. Not my fault."

"Still, we all know where to find you. You realize some of the guys are calling you James Bond, right?"

"Nice. I wonder who gave them that idea?" He stared accusingly at Damons in the rearview mirror.

Damons laughed the incredibly infectious laugh he was famous for. It was hard for Tope not to join in, but today he just wasn't feeling the joy. His uncle was dead and Tope hadn't had a chance to say goodbye. The ache in his gut was far stronger now, despite the fact that Jack Baker had been gone for more than two years. With the stress of discovery behind him, Tope felt the loss of his uncle and best friend far more keenly than he'd previously allowed himself. Grief was a luxury on these operations, one he could not afford at the time of Jack's death.

The constant stress of his cover was over and the holes left in his psyche would be filled with loss. How could the world keep turning, people continue to live and to love without Jack in it? It was impossible. The world had to have Jack in it. But it didn't and the void that loss created was immense. He needed to find this Sawyer Kingsley and thank him for not giving up on a difficult murder case. Maybe he'd travel for a while and head out to Iowa and meet up with him, tell him thank you, and visit Jack's grave. Maybe he'd do that.

Tope's thoughts were shattered as his eyes came to rest on a familiar face in the car next to them. There *had* been perps that got away, and Tope was staring into the angry eyes of one of them. Now Tope was the hunted one. He saw the glint of a gun through the window and yelled to Damons.

"Move it!" he screamed, as he raised his gun and fired through the window.

No questions asked, Damons hit the gas and burned down the street, speeding in and out of traffic as storefronts and stop lights sped by. The car beside them slipped into the lane behind Tope and Damons, following closely behind them. Shots were fired from the car in pursuit as Damons continued to focus on the road ahead while avoiding the bullets that zinged through the car. Tires screeched and the rain battered the windows, making it difficult to see behind them.

Keeping as far to the side door as possible, Tope saw the back window shatter as a hail of bullets passed through. The sound of police sirens filled the air as local law enforcement joined the chaos and raced after the two cars. Civilian cars pulled to the side as the bullets were fired, obviously attempting to stay as far out of the way of stray gunfire as they could on short notice.

    Apparently thinking better of the gunfight, the trailing car sped down a side road and two police cars followed them, tires screaming as they fought the slick, wet roads. Once the shooters were gone, Damons slowed down and pulled to the side of the road holding tightly to his left shoulder.

Chapter Two

"Damons! You're hit!" Tope jumped out of the car on the driver's side and pulled the driver's door open. He started to help his friend from the car.

"Stop right there." Surrounded by D.C. police officers, Tope realized he and Damons were basically in the middle of another sticky situation…one that could go south if someone breathed wrong. His suspicions were confirmed with the sound of several rifles being locked and loaded. Without huge logos on FBI vehicles, it was often hard to tell the good guys from the bad.

Tope stopped trying to get Damons out of the car and lowered the wounded man slowly back into the car while holding his opposite hand in the air.

"We're FBI. I've been undercover and my friend is hurt. He has his ID on him, I do not. I need to get him to the hospital right now. He's bleeding badly."

With great effort, Damons reached into his coat pocket and pulled out his badge, handing it to Tope.

"Here," Tope called to the officers, "here is his ID." The officers never lowered their guns, but one moved forward and reached for the badge wallet. Tope slowly handed him the holder and the officer looked at it, immediately lowering his rifle.

"FBI," he said flatly, calling behind him. The others lowered their rifles as well and headed back to their cars. "I wish you feds would file a flight plan or something before putting innocent people at risk with your car chases."

"Surely you noticed we were being chased, not chasing. As 'feds,' we try really hard to be more organized with our surprise shootings." Tope smiled sarcastically. "Now, if you're done with us, may I please get my partner here to the hospital?"

The words had no more than left his mouth, when he heard the ambulance sirens coming up behind them.

"Us 'local' types are pretty adept at calling an ambulance," the officer replied with equally as much sarcasm.

Tope dropped his head, feeling sheepish. He hadn't started the exchange, but he sure didn't need to jump in the middle of it. He looked up and stuck his hand out to the officer. "I apologize. Thank you for your assistance. We'd probably both be dead if it weren't for you boys."

The officer smiled and shook Tope's hand. "Happy to help when we can, sorry my temper got the best of me." He returned to his cruiser as a gurney was wheeled to the side of the car. Tope stepped back, giving them room to remove

Damons from the car. The officers had evidently also called a tow truck and it arrived just as Tope was following the gurney to the waiting ambulance. With instructions shouted to the tow truck driver to deliver the SUV to the FBI evidence lot, he climbed into the ambulance and they left for the hospital with lights flashing and siren blaring.

"I wasn't actually bleeding to death, you know. It's just a graze. It was just ever so much more fun to watch you insulting the local LEOs, so I thought I'd just keep quiet." The gurney was set so Damons was sitting up, smiling smugly at his friend.

"Nice. I just hate it when those guys get lippy. What are we supposed to do? Tell the bad guys to stop chasing us, so we can get out of the car and kindly work together and find a safe place to blow each other away? We didn't exactly have time to get out of traffic."

"They know that. When a chase ensues, it just makes their job harder. We have to understand that. Sometimes they blow our operations, innocently trying to help. It happens."

"Yeah, yeah. You feeling okay then?" Tope stretched his neck to see the bandage job on Damon's arm.

"No. I feel awful and I want ice cream and pudding for a week. I want a cushy hospital room with gorgeous nurses waiting on me hand and foot, and on whatever else I may possess that they can think to wait on. I suppose I'm going to have to settle for three hours in an emergency room with overworked doctors and nurses hurrying to the next trauma. No pudding or ice cream. Nice. I deserve better."

Damons laid his head back against the bed and closed his eyes. Tope had to chuckle.

"You're such a girl, Damons."

"Better not say that to my girlfriend. She resents that stereotype, however much she may agree with you."

The EMT who was keeping an eye on Damons vitals chuckled softly.

"Look on the bright side," smiled Tope. "You're gonna get a week off with pay, and I'll bring you ice cream and pudding when I visit. How's that?"

"Better than nothing, I suppose."

By this time the ambulance was pulling into the hospital and the attending EMT was shaking his head. "This is the most fun on an ambulance ride I've had in a long time. You two banter like you're married." He chuckled as the back doors opened and the gurney was pulled from the ambulance and wheeled into the ER.

Several hours later it was long past dinnertime and Tope was walking Damons to a waiting taxi. With the SUV in evidence, neither man had a car.

"I'm starved," said Tope. "Wanna go get some ice cream and pudding?"

"Sounds good to me."

Tope instructed the driver where to drop them. The taxi rolled up in front of the restaurant and he helped his friend out of the backseat. They strolled into their favorite Italian spot and were seated right away. They enjoyed a light dinner, with Damons expressing relief in each bite that he'd been hit in his left arm, leaving him still able to eat, drive and fill out massive amounts of agency paperwork. That last part was spoken with not as pleasant a face as the first two items.

Tope put in a call to the team leader, Patrick Richards, to let him know he was feeding the injured agent and they would be in within the hour. He asked if Patrick would mind sending a car to get them, as theirs was now in evidence lockup. While they finished their meal, Tope watched out the window for their ride to arrive.

The rain was letting up and it looked like they wouldn't have to make a run for their ride. D.C. always smelled nice after a good rain, but the rain itself was no fun to be out in. It wasn't a long wait, and soon they were on their way to the office. Tope was already memorizing his well thought out and precise list of reasons why the damage to the SUV couldn't be blamed solely on him. In the end, he decided it sounded like one long whine and he'd simply sit quietly while Patrick paced and lectured him on the fine points of responsible use of agency resources.

Their driver was instructed to drop Damons off at home for some well-earned days off and Tope was returned to the field office. Patrick's lecture didn't last as long as usual, and soon Tope was given the props he deserved for a job well done during the last eighteen months.

"I know this time was rough on you, losing your uncle like you did and having to stay planted in the op." Patrick was sitting at his desk now, his arms resting on the desktop, his fingers laced.

The only difference between Patrick and his brother Cayman was pretty much the color of his eyes. Patrick had blue eyes and Cayman had those green eyes that made the secretary pool swoon every time he walked by. Both men looked like they'd just come from a Beach Boys concert having been *in* the band. However, it being early spring and all, there was no tan.

"It's all good," smiled Tope. The smile was genuine, but still masked the pain he couldn't bring himself to share just yet. "I lived, and I'll spend some time in Iowa over the next few months, saying goodbye."

The office door opened and Cayman Richards strolled in. Tope stood and shook his hand and Cayman sat down in the chair next to him, smiling widely.

"That's just what we wanted to discuss with you." Patrick nodded to his brother and began. "We know your cover was blown. We haven't figured out how that happened yet, but we know every mob hit man is going to be hot on your trail. We already have agents watching your apartment, just in case someone decides to make a mess of your things. But we need to get you out of Dodge, if you know what I mean."

"Yeah, I figured."

Cayman spoke next. "You've done a great job on this op, and I'm sure once we determine the leak, we'll be better able to determine what is next for you. For now, Patrick, Andre, and I have decided a six-month hiatus might be just what you need. You mentioned you wanted to go back to Iowa…Blakely, is it?"

Tope nodded.

Patrick picked up the conversation from there. "We want you to take a couple weeks off, fly back there, get settled in and then we want you to work in a consulting capacity with the local

LEO's in Blakely. You may not be needed at all, but if you are, you are to make yourself available to them. Are you willing to do that?"

"I can do that." Tope was shifting uncomfortably in his chair.

"I hear a 'however' coming," smiled Patrick.

"Well, Blakely is a pretty small place compared to D.C. How long do you think I'll need to stay there?"

Patrick and Cayman shot quick glances between them. Cayman answered Tope's question. "You'll be there until we are certain it's safe for you to come back to D.C. We'll have to get some confirmation from our informants and find out how much damage control we need to do, and once we've determined how much and how soon it can be accomplished, we'll contact you. In all honesty, Tope, it could be a minimum of six months, thus the hiatus."

"Six months! With local LEOs? Come on guys, could you do that?" Tope was worried he'd completely lose his edge if he stayed in small town America too long.

"It's not a question of 'if' we could do it or 'if' you could do it, Tope. It's what we're telling you to do. When the problem is solved, and we feel you're safe, we'll call you back to D.C. It may not take six months, but again, it might. Just help out where you can and hang in there. We won't forget our best agent is missing from the group, trust me."

"Okay, I'll do it. But, yeah, don't leave me hanging out there too long."

Cayman paused before speaking again. "There's something else, Tope."

"Okay, you sound ominous. Again."

"Do you remember the Manning case?"

"The spy fiasco? Are you talking about Miriam Manning? The woman who stole classified information and sold it to the Russians?"

"Yes." Cayman sat back in his chair.

"She fried for that, right?"

"She did, and she had a husband and daughter. Do you remember that?"

"Not so much, but sort of. It's been a long time ago, one of those cases we studied in school."

"Well, they disappeared off the face of the earth. No one ever heard from them again after her death. The husband was always a suspect in the case. They thought he was working with his wife, but no one could prove that. We're wondering if the daughter got caught up in it as she grew. Maybe her father groomed her for the 'family business' kind of thing. When you come back, we're going to put you on that case again. There are some things that have come up that are a little hard to explain. I just want you to be aware, maybe study up on it while you're gone and see what you think." Cayman handed Tope a small flash drive. "This is the meat and potatoes of the case. Review it in your spare time."

"What's come up? What do you mean 'hard to explain'?"

"Just review the file. I don't want you to work on it alone, it could be too dangerous for one agent. So, keep the drive in a safe place and have a look at it when you're bored. That's all. Just have a look."

Tope shrugged and examined the drive. "I can do that, but it seems like a waste of time if I'm not here working on it."

Cayman and Patrick exchanged quick glances. "I'm just saying, have a look."

"I can do that."

The meeting was over and Cayman told Tope that his apartment was being emptied as they spoke. Tope's belongings were being brought to the field office where he could pack some things for a few nights in a hotel outside D.C., then catch a flight to Iowa in three or four days. He considered driving, since he had time to burn, and thought he might enjoy the scenery for a bit. He was in no particular hurry to get to 'Smallsville.' If he drove, he'd definitely need a different car, of course, and was assured the Bureau could help with that. The remainder of his belongings would be shipped to Blakely when he was settled in.

Within the hour, Tope was going through boxes of his belongings in the storage garage, trying to figure out on the fly exactly what he would need. They'd done a good job of organizing his most frequently used bathroom items; brush, comb, toothbrush, etc. but he still had to make some choices. It was hard to know what he needed when it wasn't hanging in an open closet before him, but he did his best. "Guess I'll buy there what I can't find here," he muttered to himself as he looked hopelessly from box to box. His furniture would be wrapped and moved to a storage facility along with his boxes once he was out of town.

Tope was dropped at his hotel and shuffled to his room complete with bodyguards placed strategically around his assigned floor. Getting out of town seemed the best solution at this point. He was certain he'd not last long with an entourage. He just wasn't the entourage kind of guy.

Chapter Three

It was a beautiful spring day in Iowa as Sawyer Kingsley knelt on one knee beside the grave of his friend, Jack Baker. The sun was shining on the emerald green grass surrounding each headstone, and the smell of freshly cut lawn filled the air. Sawyer's son, Jack, moved back and forth, semi-balanced and wriggling on the other knee. Sawyer bent over and pulled a couple weeds from the grave and sighed, dropping them to the ground.

"This is your namesake, Jack. He was daddy's best friend in the whole world." Jack looked up at him with his mothers deep brown eyes and grinned, mumbled something garbled and clapped his hands. He squirmed off of his father's knee and slid to the ground. Sawyer helped balance the little one on chubby toddler legs, before releasing the boy to wander around the area. "Stay close to Daddy, Jack."

Sawyer stood and watched his son with pride as he spoke to his friend. "Just look at him,

Jack. Isn't he something? Who'd have ever thought this would be my life?" He smiled sadly and studied the headstone. "I always thought you would be a part of this. You'd like Esley, you know. She's amazing. But then, I guess you know all about her, including how she looks in her underwear…considering it was you who hid her in that bale of hay." He pulled a piece of gum from his shirt pocket and unwrapped it, stuffing the wrapper back in his pocket and the gum in his mouth, chewing softly. Baby Jack, hearing the noise of the wrapper, rushed to his father's side and ran into his legs, wrapping both arms around them.

"Me! Me!" he cried, letting go of his father's legs. He stepped back so he could better see Sawyer's mouth and pumped his fingers into and out of a fist as he reached upward. Sawyer chuckled. "You know you can't have gum." The child's face clouded over but soon broke into a wide smile as his dad took a small sucker from his pocket. Jack jumped up and down, clapping his hands and giggling at the sight of the candy.

"Oh, so *this* is what you want, eh? You know, if your mommy were here she'd shoot me where I stand. She doesn't think you eat this stuff, you know. It will be our little secret, right?" Sawyer finished unwrapping the sucker. "At least until you're old enough to spill the beans."

A soft melodious voice giggled behind him. Sawyer turned to see his beautiful wife standing behind him with her arms folded, the breeze gently playing in her dark brown hair. She shook her head, her smile betraying the irritated look on her face. "Yeah, it would help if you wouldn't put candy wrappers in his little pockets. You're busted. Where's my gun?"

Sawyer grinned and turned back to their son. Esley moved to his side and slid under his arm, snuggling into him, watching Baby Jack squatted down, seriously studying the grass. "I have groceries in the SUV, but thought I might find you here. I stopped when I saw your car."

The two young parents watched their son play in the dirt with one hand and hold desperately to his sucker with the other.

"He's just like you, you know," she sighed. "Handsome, smart, kind, handsome, compassionate, good natured, handsome. Did I say he was handsome?" She smiled up at Sawyer.

"No, you didn't. You think I'm handsome?" Sawyer gave her a soft squeeze.

"No, I think our *son* is handsome."

"Oh, so that's how it's gonna be, is it?" Sawyer grabbed her, tickling her sides and wrestled her to the ground. Esley cried out with laughter writhing and turning, trying to escape his hands. "Stop! Stop! I can't breath!" Jack toddled over and fell on his mother's stomach, laughing and getting his sucker caught in her jacket.

"No, not the jacket!" she moaned. "It has to be dry cleaned." She pulled the sticky treat from the fabric and Baby Jack grabbed it, stuffing it into his mouth before she could take it away. She laughed at him as he wobbled away, happy with his now fuzzy sucker. Sawyer pulled her to her feet and kissed her.

"I'll pay for the dry cleaning. Promise."

"You certainly will, mister." She tried to look miffed, but clearly wasn't. The couple stared down at the headstone, their smiles gradually fading. "You miss him."

"Like I'd miss my right arm." Sawyer's gaze remained fixed on the headstone, wishing it wasn't a headstone but a door into Jack's house and they could walk inside and sit down for a drink and a visit. He glanced at his wife and his smile returned. Giving her another squeeze he guided her out from between the headstones to where Baby Jack was now staring at something squirming in the grass.

"We need to get more bugs, it would seem," giggled Esley. "They keep him almost as quiet as food!"

Sawyer bent over and placed his hands on his knees. "What you got there, buddy?"

Jack's large eyes looked up and studied his father for a split second. Then, turning back to his subject, and in a low monotone, he said, "A bug a bug a bug."

Sawyer and Esley laughed as Esley leaned down and picked up Jack's tiny hand. Sawyer took the other one and they lifted Jack into the air, swinging him forward and back. Peals of baby laughter filled the air of the cemetery. The little family strolled slowly from Jack's grave, sad and grateful all at the same time. Except for Baby Jack. He felt only happiness. His laughter was musical as he cried out his only demand. "Again! Again!"

Baby Jack had a good grasp of some words for his age and along with that, he also knew a little sign language to help until the words came easier for him. Still, the few words he spoke were clear enough for Sawyer and Esley to at least interpret.

Sawyer and Baby Jack followed Esley home where Sawyer helped his wife put the groceries away before heading into the station. He was waiting on some DNA results in a case he'd been prepping for court and wanted to see if they'd come in. However, the day before, he'd announced to the station that he was taking the day off today, didn't want any calls and definitely wanted to have some family time. He needed that and Esley and Baby Jack needed that. Sawyer felt that most likely no one would call him for with DNA results that could wait until he was in again. He'd made his position pretty clear. His curiosity getting the best of him, he thought he'd run in and check to see if the results were in.

It was a quiet day at the station, a rare occasion for sure, but Captain Amerson was in and motioned for Sawyer to come to his office. Sawyer made his way through the workstations in the bullpen and opened the door.

"What's up?"

"Have a seat," said the captain. His voice took on a casual tone as he leaned back in his chair and placed his hands over his head, lacing his fingers together.

Sawyer sat down and looked expectantly at Amerson. It wasn't uncommon for them to meet and shoot the breeze, especially on a day when neither was supposed to be in the office. But somehow, the air in the room felt like this conversation was going to be different.

"You've had three partners since Jack died, am I right?"

"Well, two. You can't count Esley."

"Yes I can. I'm your captain and I assigned her to you. I can't help it if you married her. She was still one of your partners. The other two, well, let's just say they didn't work out. Agreed?"

"Agreed." Sawyer shifted in his chair uneasily. "This isn't going to be about finding me another partner, is it? I'm doing quite well on my own."

"Yes, you're doing very well, however, you need a partner."

"*Why*? I'm getting the work done, cases solved, attending court hearings when needed. And I'm prepared for those hearings, as well. How is a partner going to make things go smoother? There'll never be another Jack. You know that."

"Yes. I'm painfully aware of that fact." Captain Amerson sighed and leaned forward. "However, there's been a 'development' and you're getting a new partner. This partner will be temporary, not really a partner so much as a consultant."

"A consultant? How does that work? I need a consultant?"

"No, this man needs a place to hide out for a few months. He's FBI, one of their best agents, as I understand. He's been working undercover and his cover was blown just as the bust was made. He needs to leave D.C. and he's on his way here as we speak."

"What am I supposed to do with a consultant, an FBI consultant, at that? Are you kidding me? This is ludicrous. You know the Feds are just looking for a hideout. Send him to Bolivia. A guy can easily disappear in Bolivia. Why Iowa? Why Blakely?"

"Because he needs to spend some time with you."

Sawyer stared blankly at his captain. "You lost me."

"The man's name is Tope. Tope Daniels. He is Jack Baker's nephew. The op he was involved in prevented him from coming to Jack's funeral or he would've been here. He's due in tomorrow and I need you to be nice."

"Yeah, but why does Jack's nephew need to spend time with me?"

"From what I understand, he wants to thank you for finding Jack's killer. He was very close to Jack while they were growing up. You'll understand more when he gets here, or so I'm told."

"As far as I'm concerned, Mr. Daniels needs to contact my cousin, Grant. You and I both know it was Grant who connected those very important dots and found the killer. Send him to Denali Park. I'm sure he'd totally love Alaska."

"He's coming here. He's driving out, spending some time alone with his thoughts, I guess. He's been on the road for a couple weeks now. He's been taking it slow, enjoying the drive and will arrive here tomorrow, like I said."

Sawyer stared into space. "How does that work? His nephew is old enough to be an FBI agent? That doesn't seem possible. Jack spoke fondly of a nephew of his, but I was thinking of a kid half Jack's age." His eyes took on a look of discovery. "Oh, no you don't. NO you definitely don't. I will not be a babysitter for a naughty new FBI agent that has had his hand slapped and then was sent into hiding. No way. I'm not a babysitter.

Find yourself another man. There's not a chance in-"

"Tope Daniels is your age. He was a couple years younger than Jack. You can ask him about that when he gets here, as I'm not clear on how all that came about and I don't really care. This guy doesn't have a lot of options. He needs to be lost for a while."

"Bolivia. Did you not hear me? I'm sure they have wonderful babysitters in Bolivia."

Captain Amerson shot Sawyer one of his famous warning looks. "Get over yourself. You're not babysitting. He's an accomplished undercover agent."

"Really? Then how come he has to go into hiding? Obviously, his cover was blown. He can't be that good."

"Listen to me, Kingsley. I said, get over yourself and I meant it. He needs some friends right now, and if I were him, I wouldn't want to have to punch my way into a forced partnership. He's no happier about this than you are. Deal with it. Fast. Dismissed."

"But Captain, I-"

Captain Amerson stood and in his most cordial voice repeated his command. "I said *dismissed*." He sat back down and began signing the stack of documents on his desk.

Sawyer sighed and stood. He started to speak again and Amerson held up a flat palm, never lifting his eyes or his pen from the paperwork. Sawyer turned and left the office.

He checked his box for DNA results and they weren't there. He hurried to his car and headed home.

❖ ❖ ❖

Tope was enjoying his trip to Iowa. It was not too early in the spring to be rainy and wet in most places, and not so close to summer that it was hot or muggy. It was perfect weather, and he felt like he could finally breathe again. He'd had no idea how suffocated he felt during those last few months of the op. Getting himself out of D.C. and into beautiful countryside was just what his psyche needed and he relished it. Riding with the windows down and the smell of green, of trees and cattle, cleaned out his olfactory glands and brought a much needed new perspective. He found himself wondering how he'd not allowed himself this pleasure long before now. However, he made a promise as he drove that he'd never let that happen again.

He'd stopped for the night in a medium sized town along the freeway, found a hotel and acquired a room. It was nice and enough floors up that he could see the whole area. Tope thought about his assignment, kind of half vacation and half work. Staring out the window in his room, he wondered what a small town like Blakely would have that could possibly keep him busy. All he knew was that it was a country town and he'd enjoyed it when he was a kid, palling around with Jack. But Jack wasn't there anymore, the town must have changed in the past years, and he wasn't sure he could be in Blakely without Jack. Jack *was* Blakely.

Face it, Jack was everything. Tope closed the curtains and undressed by his bed. The curtains kept the spring light out and would allow him to sleep as long as we wanted. That was a good thing. He was on vacation and in no hurry to get anywhere, especially a place called Blakely, with no Jack in it.

Chapter Four

"I think Tope Daniels is arriving today," said Sawyer as he kissed Esley on the cheek. He picked up his son and threw him into the air. Over the squeals and peals of laughter he said, "Would you be up to having him over for dinner?"

Esley smiled and poked him in the ribs. "Really? You're giving me one day to meal plan? You know I'm lousy at entertaining."

"I know no such thing. And it doesn't have to be anything fancy anyway. Just spaghetti and garlic bread will do." Sawyer placed Jack on the floor and patted his behind with a smile.

Esley's brows furrowed as she sat down at the table. Resting one elbow on the table, she placed her chin in her hand, rubbing it pensively with her pointer finger. "Spaghetti, you say. Isn't that the stuff with the long noodles? Round? Red sauce and a little hamburger? Have I got that right?"

"Very funny," laughed Sawyer. "Cute."

Sawyer bent down and kissed Esley goodbye and left for work, closing the door behind him. The anticipation of meeting Jack's nephew was a mixed bag of emotions for him. Was he anything like his uncle? What was Sawyer supposed to say to the guy? He wasn't currently working on anything, so what was Tope going to do all day? All questions and no answers. Sawyer would just have to wait and see.

He pulled into the station parking lot, parked the car, and went inside. Taking the stairs two at a time, he hurried to the second floor and made his way to his office. Sawyer rarely took the elevator.

After solving the last murders with his cousin, Grant Mulvane (murders that included the death of his partner, Jack), he was given his own office. That was mostly because in solving the two murders he was assigned, he and Grant had also solved a third murder in another county. Since the budget was pretty much carved in stone as far as raises were concerned, Captain Amerson had cleared out one of the rooms used for storage and given it to Sawyer for his good work. He'd barely gotten into some badly needed paperwork when there was complete silence in the bullpen. He looked up and into the eyes of Jack Baker. It wasn't *really* Jack, but it was incredibly hard to know that at first glance.

❖ ❖ ❖

It was late afternoon when Tope arrived in Blakely. He went right to the cemetery, having called the caretaker earlier and gotten directions to cemetery itself, and to his uncle's grave.

He pulled into the parking lot, put the car in park and turned off the motor, giving himself a moment to consider what he was about to do. This would be goodbye. It would be the final reality that Jack was gone, and his gut wondered if this was what he wanted to know. Jack was really gone.

With a sigh, Tope lifted the handle and pushed open the car door. It had to be done. He felt like his shoes were filled with cement, each step taking a horrendous effort. Still, there was a sense of subdued anticipation, a sense of needing to know it had happened. Stupid, really. His brain new it was real, his heart wished it wasn't.

He counted the rows of headstones and when he came to the row that would house Jack's remains, he knew exactly which one it was.

Down the row stood a beautiful, grand headstone with fresh flowers at its base. Tope turned and strode the short distance to the site. He read the words at the top of the headstone. "Having given all he could give, our friend now rests in this place. Missed every day, and never forgotten."

Another deep sigh escaped from Tope. This would be goodbye, and where was he to start?

"More my brother than my uncle, Jack. You know that, right? I'm sorry I wasn't here to keep you safe. I'm sorry you had to go in such a violent way. I'm sorry...I'm sorry for my loss. Selfish, eh? But I am. I'm sorry for me, because you were such a big part of who I am. You always will be, Jack. Always."

With his hands in his pockets he stood beside the grave and thought of all the goofy times they'd had as kids. He regretted not continuing those summer visits even after they'd grown. They both could've taken vacation time. *Why didn't I do that? Why didn't I force the issue and keep those summers special, like they were when we were kids?* It didn't matter, and he knew it was a waste of time and energy to try to fix what was unfixable.

He rubbed a finger over his forehead. "I've gotta go meet your buddies now, Jack. I'll do my best to not disappoint you." He chuckled softly. "You'd have some dumb thing to say right now, I know it. But I will do my best to make you proud."

Tope returned to his car with feet that felt a little lighter, and a heart knowing now what his brain had always known. The sadness was real, the loss was intense, and they would fade in time, at least he hoped that would be the case. But the memories would always be his. Climbing back into the car he stuck the key in the ignition and continued to the police station.

Tope opened the door of the station and hurried up the stairs, not wanting to take the time to find the elevator, which he knew couldn't be far. However, he wanted to get this introduction over with and move on to this mini vacation he was taking. He hadn't expected the reception he got when he walked into the office.

The usual noise and chatter ceased immediately as he entered the room. He gazed around the desks and cubicles uneasily, as all eyes landed on him with shocked gasps.

"Uh, I'm looking for a Captain Amerson," Tope said, slowly scanning the room. No one moved, or made any attempted to direct him. They stared at him like he'd suddenly turned them all to stone with his glance. *Small town, local LEOs, yup. I pretty much nailed it in that meeting with Patrick and Cayman.*

He thought maybe these folks didn't get out much. Tope raised his eyebrows and changed the statement to a question, "Captain Amerson's office?" Several hands pointed to his left amidst stunned stares. A door opened and he looked up as the captain walked into the bullpen.

Tope cleared his throat and made his way to the gentleman in the captain's uniform, who was also staring as if Tope forgot to dress before coming to the station.

"The resemblance is amazing," he said shaking his graying black head. His dark eyes took in every inch of Tope, leaving the new guy feeling like he'd just had an x-ray. Amerson stuck his hand out awkwardly, "I'm...I'm Captain Amerson. I had no idea you'd...you'd look so much like...like Jack. I'm stunned, as is the rest of the department."

Realizing the noise of the bullpen was still blatantly absent, he turned to the office and said, "This is Tope Daniels, everyone. He is Jack Baker's nephew. He will be working with us in a consulting capacity for a few months."

Heads nodded and a few murmurs of 'welcome' and 'hi' managed to escape still stunned lips, but gradually the noise in the room returned to its previous level.

"Let me introduce you to Sawyer. You'll be working with him almost exclusively; he'll report to me." They headed the short distance down to the end of the room and around the corner to Sawyer's office. "You may not know this, but Sawyer and Jack were like brothers. You more than resemble your uncle." Tope nodded in the affirmative. "Yes, well, it's going to take a minute for Sawyer to process your arrival, if you know what I mean."

"I understand."

They came around the corner and stood in Sawyer's doorway. Sawyer looked up and his jaw dropped. Amerson began the introductions quickly. "Kingsley, this is Tope Daniels. He'll be working closely with you in a consulting capacity on any investigations you are assigned."

Sawyer sat back in his chair, still dumbfounded. "*You're* Jack's nephew? Are you sure you're not his twin brother? I mean, just *look* at you."

Tope smiled and looked at the floor for a minute. "I never thought my resemblance to Jack would be that big an issue. Guess I was wrong."

Sawyer stood and came around his desk. "You don't just look like Jack, Tope. You're his twin. You have to understand, in this office, Jack was…he was…well, he was like a brother to all of us, but especially to me. It will take some getting used to, having you around. Expect the stares to diminish over time, but it *will* take time. Welcome to the station." He stuck out his hand and shook Tope's vigorously. "My wife is expecting you for dinner. Do you have any plans?"

Tope smiled. He was going to like this guy. "Nope. No plans. I would enjoy getting to meet your wife."

"We also have a son. I hope you're not offended, but his name is Jack." Sawyer smiled and Tope's face split in half with a wide grin.

"Why would I mind? I can only imagine how proud Jack must be."

Captain Amerson clapped Tope on the back. "It's good to have you here. I'm afraid after Jack died Sawyer had a very tough time breaking in a new partner. He married the first one I sent him, and after that he broke them into little sticks and burned them."

Tope laughed heartily. "I'll remember that."

"Oh come on," said Sawyer, "I wasn't that bad, was I?"

"You were that bad, and more."

Captain Amerson excused himself and returned to his office, closing the door behind him. Sawyer motioned for Tope to have a seat and he returned to his chair. He shook his head as he sat down and saw Tope sitting across from him. "It's just uncanny how you two look so much like each other. Let me see if I got this straight. Your mother was Jack's sister, is that right?"

"Yup. Jack was three when I was born."

"My wife is going to go crazy when she sees you."

"Excuse me?"

Sawyer had to explain about Esley's abduction and subsequent rescue. He explained how someone who called himself 'Jack' carried her through the snow and placed her in some hay he'd pulled from a large rolled bale. He also told Tope how he'd gone looking for Esley that day, and a distinct voice directed him right to her, and how Sawyer knew that was Jack.

"Doesn't surprise me in the least," said Tope, a sad smile brushing his lips. "He was a good man. The best."

"Yes. Yes he was, and I miss him every day. I do, however, promise not to break you into little sticks and burn you. Just between you and me, I think Amerson was over stating things a bit."

"That remains to be seen, now doesn't it?" The men laughed.

"Let me show you around the place. It's certainly not a D.C. Field Office, but it's ours."

"I'd appreciate you keeping that under your hat."

"Sorry, I shouldn't have said that. Good thing the door was closed."

Sawyer stood and came around his desk, heading to the door. Tope followed him out through the bullpen and onto the official tour. It didn't take long, and soon they were back in Sawyer's office. The silent stares and sudden stillness in the pen every time they walked through made Tope uncomfortable.

"I suppose at some point I'm going to have to address my likeness to Jack with them," he said, closing the office door behind him.

"Oh, I don't know, I think they'll get used to it. You don't have to say anything, but it's certainly up to you. Let's go introduce you to Baby Jack, and of course my beautiful wife, Esley."

"Sounds good."

Sawyer took the long way home, showing Tope some of the town. Blakely had changed a lot since the days he and Jack were terrorizing the residents with their boyhood pranks. Once they became teenagers, they settled down more and their interest in girls became paramount to the pranks. It was good times, and Tope enjoyed the tour and the memories.

Arriving at his home, Sawyer pulled into the garage and parked the car. As they entered the house, Sawyer called to Esley who was setting the table in the dining room. "Hey Es, we're here. Come and meet Tope. She turned to see the two of them stroll into the dining room and the color drained from her face.

"It's…it's you. It really was Jack. Really."

"I told Tope all about your experience. Are you okay? You don't look so good."

Esley held out her hand and shook Tope's, then threw her arms around him and hugged him. She released him from the hug and placed her hands on both shoulders. "You have no idea how much I appreciate what Jack did for me that day. And you…you have shown me that it really was him. It was Jack that carried me to the hay and covered me over. And it was Jack who directed Sawyer to me. I…I mean, I've seen pictures, but nothing beats the real thing. It's amazing how much you look like him."

Tope shook his head, not realizing what an emotional time this would be for him. It was not just amazing to hear this story of his uncle, but it was a huge comfort to him to know Jack was being Jack, even after he was gone. It somehow lessened the sadness and the pain of losing him, and the respect for the man he'd always admired grew even stronger.

"For Jack, I would say you're welcome. He was only being Jack. I'm sure your husband can attest to that."

"That I can," smiled Sawyer, "That I can. Now are you going to feed us, or stand there staring at our guest all night. We're aging here, Es. How can I help?"

Esley shook herself out of whatever stupor she'd fallen into and blushed. "Yes, well, let me see…has he met Jack yet? I think he's in the other room playing with the new set of plastic bugs you bought him. Why don't you introduce him to Tope while I finish getting dinner on the table. We're about five minutes from done."

Sawyer kissed his wife and gave her an extra squeeze. "Call me if you need me."

Tope followed Sawyer into the room and Jack came running to his daddy. "Daddy, Daddy!" He threw himself at his father and Sawyer scooped him up and threw him into the air. Jack laughed and hollered as he flew up and over his father's head. Sawyer turned to Tope, holding Jack in his arms.

"Tope Daniels, I'd like you to meet Jack Baker Kingsley."

Chapter Five

Tope took the child in his arms and bounced him gently as he circled the living room pointing out pictures and lamps, the front yard through the window, furniture, and Jack's toys. There was an instant bond between the two of them, and Jack refused to let anyone else hold him for the rest of the evening.

Dinner went well with Jack demanding, mostly with tears and arms, that Tope sit in the chair next to him. Tope happily obliged, and the rest of the meal was quiet with good conversation and laughter.

Once the meal was finished, Sawyer helped Esley clear the table while Tope entertained Jack. Returning from the kitchen Esley carried a tray containing large slices of chocolate cake with a fresh strawberry glaze over it.

"Me! Me!" cried Jack, his fist opening and closing when he saw the cake.

"Just a minute, Jack," said his mother, patiently. "Let me sit down and I'll give you some cake."

When she tried to feed him, he turned his head away with a sharp "NO!" He immediately began demanding cake once again, but only Tope's cake. Tope had no problem with the demand and gladly shared the cake with his new little friend.

Esley laughed and watched Tope interact with Jack. "You're great with kids, you know. You'll be a great father."

"Oh, I don't know. Working the way I do doesn't lend itself to family life so much. I mean, I know there are people who have families and are agents at the Bureau, but I feel like there'd always be that element of worry."

Esley giggled softly. "When you find the right woman, all that will change. Just look at how Jack adores you. He doesn't even know you, and he's all over you. Hate to say it, Tope, but you're a baby magnet."

Sawyer laughed and nodded his head. "Have to agree with my wife on that one. However, when it comes to that 'right woman,' try to find one who doesn't know martial arts. She can be lethal in a food fight." He watched Esley with playful eyes.

Sawyer's phone rang and he stood, moving into the living room to answer it. When he returned, his face looked like he'd just bitten into something bitter. He sat down at the table shaking his head thoughtfully.

"We hadn't seen a murder in this town for ten years until we lost Jack and a family of five within a week of each other. That was the captain and there's been another murder. What's happening around here? This time it's a decorated Marine; young, in his early thirties. I guess you're not going to get a chance to be bored, Tope. We have to get to the crime scene."

"No problem. Can I take Jack with me?"

Esley laughed and wiped the baby's mouth with a warm cloth. "He'll throw a fit, I'm sure, but he'll get over it."

The two stood and Jack started right in with his protest. He raised his arms toward Tope and whined. Tope took one of his small hands and shook it gently. "Not this time, buddy. I'll be back."

The whine became full on crying as Tope and Sawyer stepped into the garage and hurried to the car. As they backed out of the garage and onto the street, Sawyer filled Tope in on his conversation with the captain.

"I don't know much about the guy, other than he's a decorated war hero from his time in Iraq. His death will hit this town hard. He was to be the Grand Marshall of the Fourth of July parade. The people were so proud to have a hero in their town." Sawyer shook his head. "Sure doesn't feel like Blakely anymore."

"Well, then, don't move to D.C. It's definitely nothing like Blakely. Six murders in what, thirteen years? That's peaceful compared to what goes on in D.C."

"I'm sure that's true. It kind of keeps things in perspective, doesn't it?" Sawyer thought for a moment, then returned to the current case. "The victim's name is Tug Carlson. From what I've heard he was a pretty decent guy. He opened his own private detective service when he returned from Iraq. Here we are."

Sawyer maneuvered the car around squad cars and crime scene tape. They were just outside of the main downtown area. A covered body lay on the sidewalk, a hand sticking out from under the plastic sheeting. Behind the scene stood one of the larger apartment complexes in town.

There were always onlookers at any crime, however, once the body was covered, the crowd usually thinned. This time was different. This time, people stayed. Men took off their hats and held them respectfully in their hands. Women covered their mouths, heads bowed, shock registering on every face. This man was a Marine, and his town loved him.

Sawyer stepped from the vehicle and proceeded to the body. Captain Amerson was there, standing beside another officer.

"Hey Captain," began Sawyer. "did anyone see what happened?"

"Not that they're saying. But there could've been someone inside the complex who saw something. I've got officers canvassing door to door to find out."

"Anybody hear anything?" Sawyer slipped into exam gloves and squatted down. He lifted the cover, studying the dead man's face.

He appeared to be mid to late fifties, graying hair and well muscled for his age. Pulling the blanket further back he saw a gunshot wound to the chest. The blood on the sidewalk ran off the edge and into the gutter, forming a puddle there. CSI was busy collecting evidence as he spoke with the captain.

"Nothing. The wound looks like the bullet came from a rifle, but if it did, it was long range. That means a hit, and the weapon had to be a sniper rifle." Captain Amerson surveyed the crowd and called to his men. "Hurry up with that tape. I want the crowed moved back at least fifty more feet. We can't afford to have any important evidence destroyed. Hurry it up!"

"A hit? In Blakely? That's a first." Sawyer shook his head and the captain responded with his signature frown.

Tope joined Sawyer at the body, also donning exam gloves. Careful to avoid the blood on the sidewalk, he leaned over for a closer look. He turned the man's head and inspected around the ears, then checked the throat. There was nothing to indicate a struggle. He studied Sawyer. "It was a clean shot, but if no one heard it then Captain Amerson was right. The shooter had to be some distance from the target, probably had a silencer."

Both Sawyer and Tope stood and surveyed the buildings around them. "That one," they said in unison. Both looked at each other in surprise. They'd pointed at the same building.

After several hours of making lists of what they needed to do and long discussions with the officers who'd interviewed tenants of the apartment building, they made plans to meet up in the morning at the office. Sawyer dropped Tope at the station to get his car and headed home.

The next morning they met as agreed and spoke to Captain Amerson, filling him in on their plans.

"We're heading to the bank building this morning and will then begin getting more acquainted with Tug Carson. I'm thinking there's a lot we don't know about the man."

"Agreed. Keep me posted. How are you doing Tope? You settling in?"

"I'm just trying to stay out of the way. Sawyer, here, seems to know his way around an investigation."

Sawyer chuckled. "Just don't stay too far out of the way. I can always use another set of eyes and ideas. We're partners, as long as you're here. Don't forget that."

"Good to know."

Amerson dismissed them and they headed to Sawyer's car.

Tope was quiet, thinking about the different points of the case, but finally asked the question that was pressing on him. "How did you know which building last night?"

Sawyer laughed. "You mean which building the shot came from?"

Tope nodded.

"I had a good friend in the Army who was a sniper. He taught me a lot about how a sniper thinks, and how he chooses his 'nest.' I gleaned some valuable information from the guy, and have used it more than you'd think in my profession."

Sawyer watched Tope out of the corner of his eye and finally asked, "How about you? Do you have sniper training or have you learned it like I did."

"I'm an Army sniper, trained and seasoned. I don't talk about it much. It's one of those things people either admire or fear you for. Best to keep it quiet."

"Yeah, I hear you."

They arrived at the bank building and Sawyer went in search of the manager. He was directed to his office immediately. Henry Fitsimmons was a short, round man with a large protruding stomach and two chins. His small dark eyes were birdlike, his dark hair looking as if he'd lost his comb weeks previous. Not the currently popular tousled hairstyle, exactly, but as Sawyer studied him for a moment, he wondered if that was the effect the manager was trying for. It wasn't working. The top of his head looked like an explosion in a mattress factory.

After Sawyer explained what he needed, the manager, a little shaken by the information, took him to the elevator. He pulled a large key ring from his pocket and put a key into the keyhole for access to the top five floors.

"Has anyone else requested access to these floors today?"

"No, sir. No one."

"Are there copies of those keys anywhere else in this building?"

"I have an extra set in my desk. It's a locked drawer-"

"I need to see those keys right now."

They hurried back to the manager's office and Fitsimmons unlocked a small drawer in the right hand side of the desk. The keys were there, just as they should be.

They returned to the elevator and Tope joined them. The manager stuck the key in the lock for the upper floors, again, and looked questioningly at Sawyer. "What floor did you want?"

"The top floor, please."

The button was pushed for the eighteenth floor and the elevator started to move.

Tope leaned against the wall of the elevator and folded his arms across his chest. "I asked around the bank to see if anyone saw anything out of the ordinary when they came in this morning. Nothing was reported. I hope you don't mind."

"Not at all," replied Sawyer. "It was worth the effort."

The elevator stopped and the men stepped out into a large, unfinished open area with smaller office buildings in the back. Picture windows looming from floor to ceiling circled the room allowing bright sunlight to warm the area.

"I'll just head back down to my office," said the manager, peeking his head out of the elevator. "You can call me if you need me." Sawyer nodded at the man and the elevator and the doors closed.

Although they knew the hit was the night before, both men drew their weapons and quietly searched the area.

"Clear," called Sawyer. Tope answered back with the same. Finding the smaller offices vacant, they holstered their guns and continued searching for signs of a shooter.

"Over here," called Tope, his blue eyes already scanning the city blocks.

"It looks like he didn't take much time for the cleanup. There's a spent shell over there and this table would've been where he set the rifle."

The small table was wooden, sturdy, probably a carpenter's table, and was certainly capable of holding a rifle still enough for a good shot. Sawyer pulled out his phone and called for a

CSI team to come to the bank. After he ended the call he went to the window and found that the shooter had a clear shot from his vantage point in the building to the crime scene several blocks to the south. There was a perfect hole cut in the glass.

"He came prepared," said Sawyer. "He had to have a glass cutter to make this hole."

"Here's the shell casing." Tope was knelt down, examining something on the floor. Sawyer took clean exam gloves and an evidence bag from his jacket pocket and picked up the shell casing, studying it in the dim light.

"A professional shooter never leaves a shell casing behind. He must have been in a big hurry, but why? The bank would have been closed at the time of the shooting. How do you suppose he got in and out so cleanly? There has to be a back door to this building, right?" Tope was scratching his head.

"There is a back door, but it is kept locked with an alarm on it. It didn't used to be, but the bank put new rules into effect several years ago regarding security, and now it's kept locked around the clock. Employees have keys to get in and out, but the door is not made available to the general public." Sawyer kept studying the large vacant area, hands on his hips.

"There is so much of this that just doesn't make sense." One could almost see the wheels turning in Tope's head. "Seriously. A hit man who leaves an empty shell casing in the nest? That's just unheard of. But not everyone can make a shot like this, at this distance. I realize it's not a mile away, but still, several blocks would take a decent marksman."

Sawyer stopped studying the floor for more evidence and turned back to Tope. "What if the guy entered the bank before it closed and hid somewhere. He could have waited until it opened, filled with customers this morning, and then walked right out the front door."

Chapter Six

Tope stared at the shell casing through the clear bag, weighing Sawyer's scenario. "Did you say the back door was locked and only employees have keys?"

"Yeah, that was my second thought."

"Beside your initial idea, there's a really good chance we could be looking for an employee. At the very least, an employee who lost their key, had their key stolen or 'loaned' their key to a friend, which would not just be stupid, but highly unlikely."

"An employee." Sawyer stared at Tope, deep in thought. "We need to do background checks on every employee, including any who were recently fired or who quit within the last year. A lock like the one on that back door has to keep a log of entries and exits and whose key was used."

They heard the elevator doors open. "That must be CSI," said Sawyer.

Although Sawyer had told him in Amerson's office they were partners, Tope felt it necessary to keep from jumping to the front of the line with each event in the investigation. He would be the junior partner here and he needed to remember that.

Leaving the CSI team to do their work, Sawyer and Tope returned to the elevator and went back down to the main floor. They went into Mr. Fitsimmons' office to request a list of current employees and any employees who quit or were fired in the last five years. They also requested a copy of the log for the back door.

"I can have that for you in ten minutes if you'd care to wait." Mr. Fitsimmons' eyes darted from one man to the other with a near wild look in them. Tope thought the little man must be pretty tightly wound.

"I'm afraid we'll have to come back for that, we've got some things to follow up on, Mr. Fitsimmons-"

"Call me Henry," interrupted the manager.

"OK, Henry it is. We'll be back this afternoon for that list, Henry."

They decided to interview people who knew Tug and began with his landlady. According to his driver's license, he lived in one of the upscale apartment complexes on Blakely's Eastside. It turned out to be a very good starting point.

They knocked on the landlady's door and a middle-aged woman with grey hair and smiling, dark eyes greeted them.

"My name is Sawyer Kingsley and this is my partner, Tope Daniels. We'd like to ask you a few questions about your tenant, Tug Carlson."

"Oh, my, such a sad thing. Yes, yes, please come in." She opened the door wider and motioned for them to have a seat. They sat down on the couch in a roomy apartment with nice furniture. The room was tidy, and the woman was well dressed, not expensively dressed, but clean and well kept. A large window let in light, eliminating the need for lamps.

"I was so sorry to hear about Tug," she continued. "Oh, and my name is Miriam. Miriam Hodgkins."

"Do you own this complex, Mrs. Hodgkins?" Sawyer pulled a small note pad and pen out of his coat pocket.

"Please, call me Miriam. Yes. I own this. My husband worked and we saved as much as we could for this complex. When he passed away two years, ago we'd just made our last payment and owned it free and clear. It was to be our retirement income, but he didn't live to see much of that. However, he left me well enough off that I am able to employ a fulltime maintenance man. I'm looking into hiring a manager as well."

Sawyer nodded. "Miriam, what can you tell us about Tug?"

"He was such a nice man. I believe he was a private investigator. He must have been very successful at it because he always paid his rent on time. I never had a minute's trouble with him. His girlfriend is still in the apartment, I believe."

"He had a girlfriend? What can you tell us about her?"

"I really don't care for her too much, but she's a nice enough person. I just feel Tug could have done so much better. I hear she worked at a bar, you know the type. She'll definitely have to move now, she's not the one on the contract, you see."

"Yes, well, can we have a look at the apartment?"

"Certainly. Let me get my keys. It's just three doors down the hall from here."

They followed Miriam's gray head as she continued telling them about Tug and all the good things he'd done for her. She had been going to ask him to manage the complex for her, but she never got around to it. "Isn't that just the way things go?" She asked. "All the good things we're going to do and we put off until one day it's too late."

The group stopped at apartment number seven and Miriam knocked on the door. "I'm never sure what her schedule is but she might be home," she muttered, referring to Tug's girlfriend. The door opened a crack and a pretty face with large blue eyes, red from tears, peeked out.

"Miss, these gentlemen are from the police. They need to get into the apartment."

The door opened all the way and Miriam returned to her apartment as Sawyer and Tope entered. The apartment was much like Miriam's with the same large window letting in the welcomed light. Like Miriam's, this apartment was clean and well cared for.

"Please, sit down." She directed them to the sofa and sat down across from them, waiting and dabbing her eyes.

Tope and Sawyer exchanged looks and Tope said, "I'm sorry, I didn't catch your name."

"Liza. My name is Liza."

Sawyer nodded to Tope and Tope took the lead. "Liza, did you notice anything suspicious happening prior to Tug's death?"

"He...he got really weird calls in the night sometimes, and it seemed like they were happening more and more often. He never told me what they were about, but after those calls he'd toss and turn all night. He wouldn't talk about it, though. At least he didn't with me."

"Did he ever say anything to you about strange things happening, other than the phone calls? Did he ever mention being followed or feeling unsafe?"

"I don't know," she said, wiping her eyes and covering her mouth with her hand. The tears from the previous night returned and she sobbed into her tissue. "He...he just became so withdrawn, telling me I should move out, that it wasn't safe to be seen with him. He said it could be dangerous for me. But nothing ever happened and I thought he was just being paranoid."

"Was he often paranoid like that or was this something new?"

"He was usually pretty even tempered. He didn't act like that until these calls started coming in. Something happened, but I have no idea what it was."

"We're very sorry for your loss," began Sawyer, "and we really hate to bother you, but we need to see Tug's room and maybe have a look at his belongings."

"I understand. It's just..." her voice trailed off as she stared out the large window. "I'm not...I can't seem to wrap my head around the fact that he's not going to walk through that door."

Realizing what she'd said had nothing to do with what they'd asked of her she stood up. "I'm so sorry, I'm afraid my brain isn't working very clearly right now. This way. Our room…his room is just this way."

They followed her down the hallway and she stopped before the door into the bedroom. "Here. This is...our bedroom." She pointed weakly into the room, but did not go in.

Tope said softly, "We'll try to be out of your hair as soon as we can. We'll give a holler if we need anything from you."

"Thanks." Liza turned, walking slowly back down the hallway and into the living room. Tope watched her go and shut the bedroom door.

"Whaddaya think?" Tope stood with his hands on his hips, scanning the room.

"Of her or the bedroom?"

"I don't know…both I guess. There's something really odd feeling about this. Am I crazy? Is it just me?"

"Not sure what you mean, but if you're talking about people telling half truths, then yeah." Sawyer was going through the drawers and finding nothing. He opened the small drawer at the top of the dresser. There was a matching small drawer beside it. In the second one he found a set of keys, which he put in an evidence bag, and a few odds and ends that didn't seem of much consequence.

"Yes! That's exactly it. I feel like I'm in some kind of freaky movie, and in a minute all hell is going to break loose."

The last word had no more than left his mouth, the sound of a gunshot erupted in the living room. They rushed from the bedroom, drawing their weapons and saw Liza on the easy chair, breathing heavily with a gunshot wound to her shoulder. A man was standing over her with a gun pointed at her head.

Chapter Seven

"*Where is it?* If you don't wanna die today, you'll tell me where it is!"

Liza started to speak and Sawyer called out as they came into the living room, "BPD! Drop the gun and turn around slowly!"

The man turned quickly, his face partially obscured by a fedora style hat, and began firing shots in quick succession as he ran the few steps to the front door and then down the hall. Tope ran after him and Sawyer stayed with Liza, calling for an ambulance.

With little opportunity for a clear shot at the perp, Tope chased after the gunman, following the sound of his footfalls. Coming around the last set of stairs Tope jumped over the side of the railing and ran through the front entrance and out to the courtyard. The assailant was nowhere to be seen.

Tope turned and ran back inside, coming to an abrupt stop just inside the door. To his left there was a small alcove where a pile of outerwear had been hurriedly thrown on the floor. The long brown coat and fedora hat lay in a pile in the corner. He'd not gotten a good look at the shooters face, due mostly to the clothes he wore, and Tope knew this coat and hat belonged to the shooter. He slipped into some exam gloves and placed the coat over his arm and held the hat gingerly between his thumb and pointer finger.

He heard the ambulance approach and waited for the EMT's to enter. With a gurney between them they rushed through the entrance door and Tope went with the two men to the apartment. They raced in, focused on their patient. Tope and Sawyer stepped out of the way and spoke quietly between themselves.

"He left this for us," Tope said, holding up the coat and hat. "Did she say anything?" He nodded to the victim.

"Not much. She said he kept asking where 'it' was and she had no idea what he was talking about. But I suspect she knew more than she was saying."

Tope and Sawyer watched as Liza was placed on the gurney and then taken out to the waiting ambulance. Sawyer stopped the gurney and spoke softly to one of the EMT's. "Do me a favor, will you? Tell the hospital we need to know of her release at least eight hours prior to her going home, and at the very least, as soon as the nurses station has been given the okay to release her." The EMT nodded his agreement and they rushed down the hall with their patient.

Miriam hurried to the apartment, eyes wide.

"What's happened?" She saw the blood on the chair and nearly passed out. Tope caught her before she tumbled to the floor and steadied her while she regained her composure. "Who's blood is that?" she asked weakly.

"Tug's girlfriend, Liza." Tope released Miriam, standing close until he was sure she was going to stay on her feet.

"Who would do such a thing?" Miriam pulled her sweater tightly around her, unable to take her eyes from the blood soaked furniture. "I heard what sounded like a gun going off, but was afraid to come out until I heard the ambulance arrive."

Tope looked down at the petite woman. "You were wise to stay put, and you may want to go back to your apartment. We haven't found the gunman yet. I'll walk you down."

Miriam's eyes widened even more and clasped her hands to her chest. "Oh, thank you. I would certainly appreciate that."

Sawyer had already called for a CSI team and backup to help canvas the complex and the area around it. The department had been put on alert.

"It doesn't look like the gunman broke in, so Liza must have known who he was and let him in." He was muttering to himself as Tope came back into the apartment.

"Did you say she knew who the shooter was?"

Sawyer looked up. "No, but I wonder if she didn't know who he was. The door wasn't breached. He was either let into the apartment, or muscled his way in when she opened the door. Did you hear anyone talking prior to the shooting?"

Tope stared at Sawyer. "No, I didn't." He sounded surprised.

"Yeah, neither did I. I'm beginning to think we were set up to think it was something it wasn't."

Tope examined the chair she was sitting in. "Or, the two of them were talking softly and had a disagreement about how something should go down. Maybe the shooter got greedy and when she wouldn't tell him what he wanted to know he shot her, not knowing we were here."

"A likely scenario. I think we were her ace in the hole. She could be more brazen with him because we were here. Girl's got some guts for sure. She could have been killed. But now, we need to know if there's anything in this apartment that will tell us what these folks were up to. If that man was the same shooter who killed Tug, then he sure wasn't trying to kill Liza. If he'd wanted her dead, she'd be dead, which takes me back to thinking the two of them set this up, especially *if* he was the shooter." Sawyer returned to the bedroom and Tope proceeded to search the living room.

Tope started with the desk, which as it turned out, was the best place. He opened the desk drawers and found nothing of consequence in them, taking each one out in turn, inspecting the contents, and feeling around inside the desk for a hidden compartment. He did that with each of the three side drawers on either side of the chair. The last drawer he opened, the center drawer in front of the chair, didn't come out easily. Rather than rip it out, he felt around inside it and found what felt like a small button on the left side of the drawer wall.

He knelt in front of the desk, trying to see if it was what he thought it was. He'd barely moved his head just a bit to the left, when he pushed on the button and a dart shot from the drawer.

"Whoa!" He shouted. "What the-"

Sawyer heard him cry out and ran down the hallway. He found Tope sitting on the floor, leaning against the drawers on the left side of the desk, staring at a dart stuck into the wall on the opposite side of the room.

"What is *that*?" Sawyer went to the wall and inspected the dart.

"You tell me," chuckled Tope, relieved to have cheated death by mere inches. "It came from this drawer, and I have no idea if there are more. If that tip is poisoned, he wouldn't need another one, and I strongly believe it is."

"We'll let CSI take care of it. I'm leaving it where it is." Sawyer eyed the desk curiously and went to have a look. He bent over the drawer. "Was there always a compartment in there?"

"I suppose so, but I didn't see evidence of it until that dart flew out. You stand on that side of the drawer and I'll stay on this side. I'm going to push the button again and see if we get another dart."

Toped pushed on the button and there was a click, but no more darts. They scanned the inside of the drawer and Tope reached in and pulled out a small drawer which had apparently popped open when the button was pushed. When he got the drawer into the light, there was a small manila envelop, small enough to hold a key. By the feel of it, that's exactly what it held.

"I'll be willing to bet it's either a locker key or a safe deposit box key from a bank." Sawyer lifted the envelop from the drawer and opened it.

A small safe deposit box key fell into his hand. "Now we just have to find out which bank this key goes to."

With officers already talking to tenants and checking apartments, Tope and Sawyer left the apartment when the CSI team arrived. They drove to Front Street and to a large office complex there. Tug Carlson's office was on the third floor of the building. The detectives needed to get a look at the clients he was currently working for, and the files he had of current jobs. He'd named his business "Investigative Services." They walked through the front office door and were met by a secretary, busy making phone calls and notifying clients of Tug's unfortunate demise. She ignored their presence for the most part, continuing her conversation, until Sawyer held out his badge and ID.

"I'm very sorry Mrs. Bradford, but I'm going to have to go. The police are here. Yes. Yes, I will. As soon as I can. Thank you. Bye."

She stood after hanging up the phone and introduced herself. Shaking Tope's hand first, tipping her head of gleaming black hair as she shook his hand. Her piercing blue eyes were sad and red from crying, but she straightened her shoulders, pulled herself up to her full five feet nine inches and began. "My name is Camille. Camille Cofford. I'm...I...I *was* Mr. Carlson's executive secretary. How may I help you gentlemen?" She shook Sawyer's hand as she finished.

"I'm Sawyer Kingsley and this is my partner Tope Daniels. We're going to need access to Tug's office."

"I'll need to see a search warrant for that, I'm sure you understand. There are still sensitive client files in there that remain active investigations."

"Yes, ma'am. Tug Carlson was a military hero. It won't take long to get the required warrant." Sawyer pulled out his cell phone and called the office. "Hey Evelyn, would you talk to the captain about a search warrant for the office of Tug Carlson? I'll need that expedited. Have one of the guys bring it down to me. I'm at Tug's office now. We're going to wait here until it comes."

He said goodbye and ended the call. Glancing around the office, he saw a waiting area and he and Tope made their way to the chairs and sat down.

Camille went back to her phone calls, paying little attention to the men in the waiting area.

"Where is your family, Tope?" Sawyer hadn't had much chance to get to know Jack's nephew. He spoke softly now, keeping the conversation private. "Do you have brothers and sisters?"

"My folks are in D.C., I usually spent time every week with them, but with the D.C. operation lasting as long as it did, it was impossible to see them at all. They know I do undercover work. They don't like it, but they tolerate it. I had to contact them before I left for Blakely and tell them I had to leave town for a few months. It was pretty hard on them. As for siblings, my mom had some issues when I was born and they were never able to have another child. I'm all they've got, so my being away for such long periods is tough on them."

"Do they know you're in Blakely?"

"Nope. No one does, only my boss at the Bureau in D.C. Things like this have to be kept tight. I couldn't even go home to say goodbye to my parents, but it's really for their own safety. If the mob knew my real name, knew who my parents are, they could make things bad for us. I just keep my whereabouts quiet."

"Jack's family moved away from Blakely years ago, I'm sure you knew that."

"Yes, I actually helped Jack get them moved. We didn't get to spend as much time together as adults, like we did when we were kids, but we never lost touch. I always let him know when I was going undercover. The thing that sucks the most about this last assignment was that I lost Jack and never had a chance to say goodbye."

Sawyer stared at his hands for a moment before speaking. "If it's any consolation, neither did I. I'm sorry that you didn't get to spend more time with him. He was like a brother to me."

"Thanks. We were more like brothers than uncle and nephew. He was a good man."

Tope turned to Sawyer. "Tell me more about Jack helping Esley. I can't tell you how much that story means to me."

Sawyer rehearsed the whole story, how Jack was just suddenly there and basically saved her life. He told him about how he was ordered to stay put at the station because of his involvement with Esley, but how he had a strong feeling to go find her and how the voice in his head directed him right to the spot. He filled in the holes that were left when he and Esley had told him the abbreviated story at dinner the night before. Sawyer enjoyed telling how her rescue came together, and how it was all because of his former partner. It made him feel closer to Jack, knowing he was helping.

When he finished, Tope was smiling. "He was a pretty amazing guy. I'll have to tell my mom that story. It will mean the world to her. She took his death pretty hard."

Tope sat back in his chair and stretched his legs, changing the subject. "You know, there is something about Tug's girlfriend that isn't right. It's not like she's lying to us, exactly, but like she's not telling us the whole truth. I have to wonder if Tug felt that as well."

"Love is usually pretty blind," replied Sawyer. "It's hard to see the flaws in the people we love, hard to think they would betray us. I wouldn't be surprised if he didn't suspect her of anything. As far as we know for certain, she isn't involved. We'll have to have a lot more evidence than our gut to make a case against her."

The office door opened and an officer walked in, scanning the room. He saw Sawyer and went to him, handing him the search warrant. Sawyer thanked him and went right to the secretary's desk.

"Here you go."

She looked incredibly uncomfortable, but nodded to the men and stood. She took them to Tug's office door and haltingly opened it, walking inside. Her arms were folded across her chest and she rubbed her upper arms with her hands as if attempting to warm herself.

Sawyer turned to her. "We'll take it from here, ma'am. Thank you for your help."

She stared at the two men for a moment. "He…he was a good man, kind and honest. He didn't deserve to die like this. He…he was so proud to have served his country, so proud to be a Marine. Tug loved America; he loved the flag and everything it stood for. He…He was good at what he did and…" her voice trailed off and she abruptly left the room.

"There's more story in there, I think," said Tope, nodding in the direction of Camille.

"I agree. There's more story everywhere we look, but no one's talking."

Chapter Eight

Sawyer and Tope started searching methodically through the office of Tug Carlson. All of the files were complete, except one. That file was stuck in the back of the client drawer with no name, and the notes inside appeared to be in some kind of handwritten code. These pages would be compared to Tug's handwriting and see if he was the one who wrote them. When they came to the billing and financial drawer, they found another file just like the first one, tucked into the back of the drawer, no name and only pages of code in the same handwriting.

"Look at these," said Sawyer, holding the file out for his partner to see. "What do you suppose he was trying to decipher? These look like experiments, like he was trying to figure out a cypher. Do you agree?"

Tope studied the pages briefly. "I don't work a lot with cyphers and codes, but that'd be my guess."

Tope put the two files in an empty box he'd found by Tug's desk. As they continued through the perimeter of the office, Sawyer searched for items out of place, odd-looking things that weren't where they should be. Tope searched the drawers, walls and closets for hidden compartments. After the desk incident, he was certain Tug had more and was very careful about opening drawers.

In the far corner of the office was a small two-drawer file cabinet that looked like it was never used. There was no lock on it; cases of printer paper, toner cartridges and boxes of pens, pencils and notepads were stacked on or around it. It almost looked invisible, and that made it especially interesting to him.

Tope stood in front of the small cabinet staring at it for a few minutes before Sawyer saw him. "What have you got there?" Sawyer started toward Tope.

In that instance Tope found what he was looking for and shouted to Sawyer. "STOP!" He backed away from the unit, still studying it. "You need to call your bomb squad, right now."

"What do you see? I don't see anything but a lonely file cabinet."

"It took me a while to find it, but there is a sensor wire coming out of the bottom drawer. It's painted the same color as the cabinet, so it's hard to see, but it's there. It could be a bomb; it could be nothing. It might not even be a sensor, but I'd rather be safe than sorry after the desk incident."

Sawyer was already on the phone calling for the bomb squad. "Good eye, Tope. Glad you saw that."

"You've heard of hiding something important in plain sight?" He pointed to the file cabinet. "That's a perfect example. It seems unnecessary to the room, like he had it in case he ever needed one. That's always a big clue to me. I'd be willing to bet there is evidence in there. Seems like something a military man would do to hide important documents or information. This guy was keeping secrets, and these secrets must be very important for him to rig explosives and darts like he did. Not only did he not want people to gain access, he was willing to kill to keep them out. Let's hope whatever he's hiding isn't destroyed when the squad disarms the device. Tug had to have a way to get into it. Maybe they'll find that."

Tope and Sawyer continued searching through the piles of paperwork and files. Stacks of closed files filled each corner of the room with active files, financial statements and bills filling two four-drawer file cabinets.

Tope's blue eyes kept going back to the small two-drawer cabinet and he ran his hand through his dark hair. "How long did you say before the bomb squad gets here?" It seemed like hours had gone by since Sawyer placed the call.

Just as Sawyer was about to answer, the bomb squad team leader, Grey Wilkins, walked into the office. "Hey Sawyer, looks like we're in the right place."

"Grey, I don't think you've met my new partner, Tope Daniels," he said, seeing Grey's look of surprise. "Tope is Jack's nephew."

Tope shook Grey's hand. "Nice to meet you, Tope." Tearing his eyes from Tope, Grey scanned the room. "Where's the object in question?"

Tope directed him to the small filing cabinet. Grey squatted down and rested one knee on the floor. He was a large man, standing over 6 feet 3 inches, Tope was sure. But he appeared to know his stuff when it came to bombs. He stood up and rested his hands on his hips. One hand came up and he began rubbing his upper lip with the side of his forefinger, deep in thought. Without disturbing any of the items on or around the unit, he stretched out his hand and leaned in against the wall in an attempt to see behind the unit, which was three to four inches away from the wall. He pointed a flashlight down through the space and grunted.

"He didn't want your average Joe in there, but he made it easy enough for someone who knows what they're doing to get in, which tells me it's not a bomb, but it could be a gas of some kind. I'm going to suit up and get some of the guys in here to help me. I suggest you clear the floor. I'll call you when it's cleared."

Tope and Sawyer followed him out. There were three team members waiting there. The two men watched as the squad donned protective gear, complete with self-contained breathing apparatus. It took a few minutes to complete the process, cinching each other's arm and leg bands and finally placing the helmet on with its thick faceplate and breathing apparatus. Appropriately suited, the team members returned to Tug's office.

Tope, Sawyer Camille started into the hallway. Camille explained there were only two other offices on the floor that were occupied. They checked with the occupants, and got everyone to the elevator. Tope, Sawyer and Camille rode down in a second elevator.

Camille kept to herself a few feet away from the detectives. Tope could tell her nerves were shot, but she seemed especially pale now. He dismissed it as more stress at a time when she didn't need more stress.

While they waited, Sawyer called the office and requested a team for Tug's office, to load up all the files and papers and bring them back to the station once the room was cleared. They were going to need to review the files more thoroughly than had been possible in their search.

Moments later Sawyer received a call from Grey that it was safe to return to the office.

Windows were opened in the inner office when they arrived and there was thick grey smoke that was slowly clearing. The team members were now in the outer office and Grey pulled a small device from one of the many pockets on his suit. As he walked back into Tug's office, he moved the device back and forth. Soon he motioned for the men to remove their helmets. After removing his, Grey came through the outer office and into the hallway.

"We got some discolored smoke out of the unit once we opened it, but it wasn't toxic. We just didn't know for sure at first, and in situations such as this, it's always better to be a little extra cautious. I'm thinking he put the smoke in there to scare off anyone who might have made it into the unit. You can go on in if you like. The unit is open and safe to look at."

Camille still seemed shaken, but she returned to her desk and sat down, trying to work, but mostly staring at her desktop. Tope stopped beside her desk.

"Are you okay?"

"No. No, I guess I'm not. It seems like I haven't had time to mourn the death of my boss and friend, and...and now this. What's going on? What's happening?"

"I believe the worst is over, Camille. I'm sorry to put you through all this, but we need to find out what happened to Tug. We need to find the person who did this." He placed his hand on her shoulder. "We *will* find whoever is responsible. We will."

Camille smiled up at him with eyes full of tears. "I know you will, and I thank you for your work. I'll be fine, really."

Her large, tear-filled blue eyes were framed in a face of perfect skin, smooth and creamy. Her black hair was layered around her face and the effect was stunning. He'd not noticed her beauty when they'd first arrived, but he was sure noticing it now. Tope smiled at her, swallowed hard, and walked quickly into the inner office.

Sawyer was pulling something from the filing cabinet and having a hard time of it. Whatever it was, it looked like a strong box of some kind, and very heavy. Tope rushed to Sawyer and helped him lift the box to the desk. Sawyer's voice was strained under the weight of the box. "This thing must weigh a ton. I can't imagine what is so important that it would require this kind of security." Sawyer stretched his back once the box was on the desk. "I can't believe that little filing cabinet could hold something this heavy. Now the question is: how do we open it? It looks like it's been sealed, possibly soldered shut. What was this guy into?"

Tope shrugged and inspected the box closer. "I'd be willing to bet that filing cabinet isn't as innocent as it looks. It's obviously far more reinforced than we can see at first glance."

Tope stood from his inspection of the strange box on the desk. There wasn't a single seam that could be pried open. The box had to have been custom made, either by Tug or by someone else. There was an obviously soldered hole in the front where a rotating combination lock had been. The lock had been removed and the hole soldered shut. It was a completely sealed cube.

"We may have let the bomb squad go too soon," mused Tope, staring at the box. "We'll have to take this to the station and have it x-rayed. Who knows if it's got it's own set of traps."

Sawyer nodded his agreement. The team arrived to clear out the office, and Tope and Sawyer used one of their dollies to carry the box to the car. They wanted it inspected by the bomb squad right away and didn't want to wait for the team to bring it back with all the other items from Tug's office. After returning the dolly to the team upstairs, Tope and Sawyer drove to the office, deposited the box with the bomb squad, and headed back down to their cars.

The two men parted in the parking lot and went home for the evening. Tope's 'home' was a nice hotel in downtown Blakely. Without knowing the layout of the town after being away for so many years, he was hesitant to rent an apartment, and as yet had been unable to find the right one anyway.

The box they'd left at the station was really bugging him. In fact, this whole case was getting more and more mysterious as time went on. Who was this Tug Carlson? What was his story? The thing that bothered him the most was the itch growing between his shoulder blades. That always meant trouble, and usually big, ugly trouble. He really hated big, ugly trouble. He really did.

Chapter Nine

In the days since Tug's death, the town had really come out in support of their beloved war hero. He was nearly as dear to the town as the American flag itself. They loved and revered him. The small mid-western town was immensely patriotic and proud of the men who served their country like Tug Carlson had.

Because of this, his death hit the town hard, especially the fact that it was ruled a homicide. As Tope drove through the streets, he saw sign after sign in nearly every window, thanking Tug for his service in the Marines, for the wonderful things he'd done for the town, and praising nearly every aspect of his life. This was a crime that needed to be placed on the top of the list and solved above all else. As Tope pulled into the station he realized finding the perpetrator was not only to bring justice for Tug, but for the whole town, as well.

The itch between Tope's shoulders was getting worse as time went by. He knew it was something about Liza, Tug's girlfriend, but had no thoughts on exactly what it was. Thus...the itch. There was something she was hiding; and that by itself, made Tope uneasy. He thought she might still be in the hospital. He would recommend to Sawyer they go talk to her again. That thought helped ease the itch, at least a little.

As Tope entered the bullpen, he made his way through the desks and cubicles. The stares were still there, but he smiled at each officer and shook some hands. He couldn't blame them, nor could he help the fact that he looked like his uncle. He decided early on to consider the attention a tribute to Jack, and it always made him smile. He continued on to Sawyer's office and found him sitting at his desk filling out paperwork from their efforts the day before.

Sawyer looked up as Tope entered. "How'd you sleep? Your smile looks a bit irritated."

"No, not irritated so much as uneasy. I just can't seem to figure out Tug's girlfriend. She's got something going on, and I want to know what it is. I think we need to go talk to her. I don't know how bad that gunshot wound was, but it looked pretty bad. She should still be at the hospital, don't you think?"

"Yeah, I suppose." Sawyer stared at the papers on his desk, obviously thinking. "I've been contemplating the whole shooting thing. She had to have let the man in the apartment. There was no break in. She must still be at the hospital because we were supposed to be notified within eight hours of her release. And certainly we'd hear from the officers guarding her if she'd been released."

"True." Tope collapsed in the chair across the desk from Sawyer. "There are so many loose ends. I need a dry erase board."

"I've got the board out and was about to start putting some of the pieces of evidence together. It's in the bullpen. Go get it and roll it in here. Let's see if we can't make some sense of this case."

Tope nearly jumped out of his chair and hurried into the bullpen. He found the board near Captain Amerson's office and pulled it into Sawyer's office.

"In a hurry, I see," chuckled Sawyer as he rose from his desk. He helped Tope negotiate the large board into his small workspace.

"This is bugging me more than the eighteen month undercover op I just finished. At least there we knew who the bad guys were."

They returned to their chairs and spent a few minutes revealing the very unhelpful details of the case. Every lead led to a dead end. The board was more infuriating that helpful.

"Did you figure out what bank box that key from Tug's office opens?" Tope laced his fingers together on top of his head trying to hide his frustration.

"Yeah, I did. It just happens to belong to a safe deposit box in the same bank where the shooter's 'nest' was found. We're going to visit with Liza first, then to the bank, as soon as I get caught up on some of this paperwork, which…" he signed the sheet in front of him with a flair, "…is now complete. Let's go."

As they walked down the stairs and to the car, Tope reviewed the events of the last few days in his head. Both men were deep in concentration, playing through the evidence in their minds. The assignment was a jumble of boxes and files removed from Tug's office, booby traps, interviews, all the things they'd been weeding around and through to get to the nuts and bolts of this case. Tope couldn't help but ask the question that had been on his mind since yesterday.

"Any word on that sealed box we took out of Tug's file cabinet?"

Sawyer stopped in front of his car with a sour look etched on his face. Tope froze with his hand on the door handle. "What? What have you heard?"

"Get in the car," said Sawyer, continuing on to the driver's side.

The doors slammed shut as both men settled into their seats. Sawyer was staring at the center of his steering wheel.

"This may be bigger than we thought. Inside that box was a two page coded paper, and it looked like some kind of a list. My guess is it's a list of names and it makes me wonder if our Marine hadn't figured out the code. If the document is comprised of leaders of government, we could be in more danger than we thought. If it's names of operatives or Special Forces military, it could be just as bad. My question is, did Tug know what it was? Was it his list? If so, where did he get it? Okay, more than one question but that's been the problem with this case. There are always more questions than answers. No matter what the answers are, we need to be very careful from here on out."

Tope studied his new partner. "You know, we have a whole department at the Bureau that specializes in breaking codes. They might be able to help us figure out what we're looking at. They're decryption programs are top of the line. "

"I thought of that. I put it into the captain's hands and let him decide how he wants this to play out. It would sure be helpful to have that cracked so we knew what we were dealing with."

"Maybe the safe deposit box will give us some good news."

The hospital was the first stop. Liza had been assigned officers to guard the door to her hospital room around the clock. Knowing what room that was, they took the elevator to her floor and found the room. Not hard, since there were two officers stationed outside the door.

Liza was awake and eating breakfast. She smiled as the detectives entered her room.

"You're looking cheerful," smiled Sawyer. "How are you feeling?"

"Like somebody shot me in the shoulder." Her voice was flat, but the smile remained on her face.

"Do you feel like answering a few questions?"

"Sure."

Tope took notes as Sawyer began the interview.

"Liza, when we were at your house the day you were shot, we were just down the hall. There was no sign of a break in, no sign of a struggle, just a gunshot. How did he get in?"

Liza was suddenly very interested in her eggs and hash browns. "He…he just…came out of nowhere. Like he'd been hiding in the apartment. Yes, just like that, like he'd been hiding somewhere inside the apartment. I didn't see where he came from; he was just all of a sudden standing in front of me."

"Liza, the door was wide open when we came down the hall. He didn't have time to open a door before we got into the living room. Can you explain that?"

"I...I..." She set her fork down on the table and buried her face in her good hand. When she looked up her shoulder slumped and more tears ran down her face. Her short brown hair laid flat on her head, obviously not styled for a couple days. Her shoulders shook with sobs and when she looked up at Tope her face was wet with tears.

"He approached me a couple of months ago. He said his name was Clyde Naples and that he worked for some people who were interested in some documents Tug had in his possession. He offered me thirty thousand dollars to find them, without telling Tug, and bring them to him. I...I didn't think Tug even knew what he had was that important, but as hard as I searched the apartment, I couldn't find anything."

"Did you check his office for the papers?" Sawyer was trying to be as gentle as he could, but needed answers.

"No, no I never did. I didn't have a key to get in, and to me, breaking in felt very illegal. I don't care how much he offered, I wouldn't break the law to get him what he wanted. The files in Tug's office were extremely confidential."

The tears that had been threatening rained down her face as she looked up at Sawyer. "If I'd known it was going to come down to losing Tug, I would never have agreed. I swear it. I feel like it's my fault Tug is dead. It's my fault."

Tope was taking notes in a small spiral notebook. Sawyer pulled a chair closer to the side of the bed. "Did Mr. Naples contact you more than that one time?"

"He was *always* calling me, or coming over when he knew I was home alone. He even came into the bar where I work. He became very threatening when I told him I couldn't find what he was looking for. He hadn't paid me anything but he acted like he had, like I was cheating him by not finding what he'd ask me to find. That day when he came over, I let him in because you were there. I felt safe until he kept insisting that I knew where the documents were and I wasn't telling him. He pulled out a gun and I thought he was just going to scare me with it, which he did rather effectively."

"Did he say anything to you other than asking where the papers were?"

"No, he just kept asking me and telling me if I didn't give them to him I was going to die."

"Liza, Tope and I were just down the hall. I know the bedroom door was closed, but if you were arguing like you say, why didn't we hear voices prior to the shooting?"

"I don't know. Maybe we were talking softer than I remember. The walls are very thin in that complex. I don't know why you wouldn't have heard us."

Sawyer studied her face. Liza was trying to tell him the truth, but there was more. Somehow he knew there was more. Whatever the deal he'd made with her, she got the short end of the stick.

Pressing her too far at this point would probably do more harm than good. He opted to keep that communication open for now, and if they needed more information later, they would come back.

"We'll need you to stay in town. We may need to talk to you again. Mr. Naples probably knows we're onto him now, but he may try to contact you again. If he does, call us immediately. Change the lock on your apartment door. We'll speak to Miriam about allowing you to stay in the apartment until the investigation is over."

Liza nodded her head and lowered her eyes again. "I was afraid if I told you this you'd think I was working for him. I guess I was in a way, but it was *for* him and not *with* him. I loved Tug, very much. If I'd told him about the offer, about this man and how threatening he was becoming, maybe Tug would still be alive today."

Sawyer leaned into the bed tray that separated him and Liza. "Liza, you have no way of knowing that, and neither do we. From what we've been able to find out so far, I doubt it would have ended any differently. It's not your fault. You didn't pull the trigger on the gun that killed Tug. The shooter pulled that trigger. You can't allow him to make you think you are responsible. You aren't."

Sawyer stood and Liza stared up at him. "Thank you." Her voice was a near whisper.

"You're welcome. We'll talk again later."

Sawyer and Tope left the room and continued on to the elevator.

"She seems genuinely sorry for a scheme that definitely didn't work out the way she'd planned." Tope was thoughtful as he leaned against the railing inside the elevator.

"Yeah, she did. It's beyond wrong to use someone like that, dangle a carrot of what they consider big money, make it sound fairly innocent, and then have it turn out like it did. It makes me want to shoot him myself."

"No lie."

Sawyer continued. "I think we can cross her off the list of suspects. She was hoping to make some money to help Tug out, and herself as well. She got caught in the middle of an ugly scheme. I think that's the total of her involvement."

"Agreed."

They got into the car and Sawyer headed to the bank. "I'm becoming more and more curious about what's in that safe deposit box."

"Yeah, me, too. How much longer will it be before we find out if there was something on that dart?"

"We'll check with the lab when we get back to the station. They should have some results for us by now. Sometimes they get so swamped I don't get a call right away."

Sawyer pulled into the bank parking lot and they exited the car, both deep in thought. They entered the bank and went directly to Henry Fitsimmon's office.

"Hello, Henry." Sawyer stuck out his hand and shook Henry's. "It's good to see you again."

"And you as w-"

A loud explosion interrupted his greeting. Bank customers and employees were screaming, alarms sounded, and panic ensued. Both Sawyer and Tope drew their weapons.

Henry stood in stunned silence, his outstretched hand now shaking.

"Stay here." Tope held out his hand to indicate Henry was to stay where he was. The two detectives ran down the stairs and found the safe deposit box vault open and the customer service teller unconscious on the floor. The room was filled with smoke, making it very hard to see into the vault. Henry was following close behind in spite of the order to stay put. When he saw his employee on the floor he rushed to the desk phone and called for an ambulance.

Sawyer knelt down and checked the pulse of the injured employee. "She's alive. Hit on the back of the head so she probably didn't see her attacker. Let's see what's happened in there." He nodded toward the vault.

Guns drawn and leading the way, the two men entered the vault slowly, moving debris aside with their feet as they went. The smoke began to clear and they found the debris they'd been trying to avoid were safe deposit boxes, blown open by the explosion. All the drawers on one side of the vault lay scattered around the floor.

"I'm almost positive, when they inventory these boxes, the only one with anything missing in it will be the box that fits our key." He coughed from the smoke in the vault. "What you wanna bet?" Sawyer cast a knowing look at Tope.

"I'm sure you're right. What's the box number we're looking for?" Tope waved his arms in front of him to clear away the smoke.

"1407."

A few of the boxes were left in their slots, but blown open by the force of the explosion. All of them had items still inside, with the exception of box 1407. That box was empty, still in the slot with the door hanging off to the side at an angle, the remnants of a plastic explosive nearly covering the number.

"I'd also be willing to bet," added Tope as they examined the box, "that they misjudged the amount of explosive they needed to open that box. Either that or they planted several charges on boxes along this wall to hide their target. At least we were ahead of them on *that* little bit of information."

"I'm sure that last idea is exactly *why* they put extra charges on the wall. I wonder if they got what they were looking for or if it's somewhere on the floor. The explosion was big enough they wouldn't have had a lot of time to find it if it was blown out of the box."

"Well, that's just perfect." Tope gazed around the room at the floor. "We don't even know what we're looking for."

A look of discovery passed over both their faces. "Unless we're looking for-" Tope was joined by Sawyer, and they both said in an excited unison, "the cypher key!" They quickly donned exam gloves and dropped to their knees. They began a systematic search through the money, jewelry, and papers covering the vault floor. The firemen arrived first but when they saw there was no fire, they were dismissed. Several officers from the BPD arrived, along with a CSI team and EMTs. The officers offered to help, but Sawyer felt too many in the vault might destroy what they were trying to find. The EMT's tended to the vault teller and CSI began dusting for prints and cordoning off the vault office area. They waited impatiently for Tope and Sawyer to finish their search.

"They must have gotten what they wanted, if it was in fact a cypher." Tope stood and continued scanning the floor, hoping he'd find a spot he missed. "It seems unlikely the perps would have found what they were looking for, though. Whatever it was must have been blown into the room."

"Maybe we were too hasty in determining what we thought it was." Sawyer's voice was thick with disappointment. "It just makes sense it would be a cypher. It has to be. But if it was, why didn't Tug have it figured out?"

Tope shook his head. "Some cyphers require special computer programs to decrypt. He may not have had what he needed for this job." He glanced around at the floor of the vault. "This is going to take weeks to figure out. An inventory of what was in each box will have to be completed, and that's going to take interviews of each box holder. Even if we had the manpower to do it, it would still take weeks."

Sawyer called to the CSI team, not so patiently waiting in the outer office. He explained to them that they hadn't found what they were looking for, that every item, no matter how insignificant, needed to the catalogued and bagged. The CSI team lead stared at him like he'd lost his mind.

"If you don't mind my asking, Sawyer," said the gray-haired man calmly, obviously holding his temper in check. "What exactly is it you think we do? Why would you need to tell us to tag and bag everything?"

Sawyer shook his head. "I'm sorry, Clayton. This case has got my brain moving in a hundred different directions. You do good work; I'm not the least bit worried. Have at it."

When they returned to the station, they went to the lab to check on the status of the dart. As it turned out, there was a poison on the dart, but they had to put it in the back of the queue, since no one was injured by it. It would be a few more days, but their best guess was a toxin, called tetrodotoxin, produced by puffer fish and it was deadly.

As they left the lab, Tope was angry. "What could have been so important, or so confidential, that Tug Carlson would kill to protect it? What if Liza had found that? We need more information on Mr. Carlson. What was he in to?"

Sawyer nodded in agreement. "He will be our next avenue of pursuit. That's for certain."

Sawyer and Tope spent the next few days interviewing bank employees, customers, and safe deposit box owners. It was long and grueling and unproductive. By the end of the fifth day, with the last of the interviews behind them, they returned to Sawyer's office, wondering if they were ever going to get a break in this case. And then to their surprise…the break came, and it was a zinger.

Chapter Ten

"You got plans for dinner?" Sawyer waited; sure his partner would have no plans. Tope had been to Sawyer's home several times since his move to Blakely and had great fun playing with baby Jack, wrestling and tickling, laughing heartily at the sounds of the baby's giggles. Sawyer began to suspect his real reason for accepting the dinner invitations was to play with Jack, not necessarily to spend time with him and Esley. Watching Tope entertain their son made both Sawyer and Esley feel like he was more and more a part of their family.

"I'm going to have to take a rain check on that, Sawyer." A sly and inviting smile split Tope's face.

"You're going to spend the night alone and sad, you know. And Jack will be none too happy about it, either."

"Now, *that* could really break a guy's heart. Why'd you have to go and say that? I'll just have to come over and play with Jack another day.

However, I definitely won't be alone and I won't be lonely."

"Okay, what are you up to? What's going on?" Sawyer masked his curiosity with a dubious tone.

"I happen to have a date."

Sawyer was shocked. "A WHAT?"

"A date. You know, where two people go out together, have a good time, maybe eat some dinner, see a movie. Surely you remember that."

"Yes, I remember that," he said flatly. "My question is mostly in regards to *who* you might be seeing. Or is that a big secret?"

"No, no secret," replied Tope, his voice aloof. "If you must know, I'm taking Camille Cofford to dinner."

"Camille Co- Tug's secretary?"

"Administrative Assistant."

"When did you have time to strike up *this* relationship?"

"I go home to an empty hotel room every night, when I'm not having dinner with baby Jack, oh, and you and Esley, of course. That gives me all kinds of time to…explore the finer points of Blakely."

"How long has this been going on?" Sawyer was happy for his partner, but concerned this relationship would interfere with their investigation. However, he knew better than that because Tope was FBI and certainly wouldn't have started up a liaison with a suspect in a murder inquiry. Camille had been cleared early on as a suspect in the case anyway, Sawyer knew that, but there was always concern. "We're partners, you know. We share everything."

"Yeah, well, this is really our first date. She was pretty shaken up by Tug's death and I wanted to give her some space, so I waited." Tope finished with the words pouring out of his mouth like water down the wall of the Grand Canyon. He was obviously attempting to justify his date. "It's been almost two weeks now, and I called to see how she was doing, and she was doing fine, so I asked her out, and there you are. We're having dinner tonight."

Sawyer was stunned, but quickly regained his composure. "Good for you! I'm glad to see you helping this poor, saddened, but beautiful, woman overcome her grief and-"

"Don't say it…let me. 'You're sure I'm just the man for the job.' "

"Right. And humble, too."

❖❖❖

It was a beautiful clear evening in Blakely with the sun just setting and dusk covering the sky. The remains of a striking sunset were just beginning to wane. When Tope picked Camille up that night, she wore a pair of black jeans and a softly flowing cream top. Her black hair lay soft and loose around her shoulders and her eyes, no longer red and swollen, were very, very blue. She was even more stunning than he remembered.

"Ready to go?" He asked, sure from the look of her she was completely ready.

"Let me grab my jacket."

Tope waited on the porch of a small but newer ranch-style home just outside the city. The house sat in the center of a nice subdivision of similarly styled homes with small yards in the front and, from what he could see, larger yards in the back. All had two car garages and beautiful Midwestern front porches.

"Sorry to keep you waiting." She hurried through the door with her coat over her arm, checking to make sure the door was locked when she shut it.

"No problem. I've been admiring the neighborhood. This is a very nice area."

They stepped off the porch and onto the front walk that led through a three-foot white picket fence. Tope helped her into the car and came around to his side, sliding into the driver's seat.

"You know this town much better than I. Do you have a favorite place you like to eat? Maybe a place you don't usually go?"

Camille tipped her beautiful head and thought for a moment. "Do you like Italian?" Her smile lit up her face.

"I do." He turned to face her, shifting his shoulders and sinking into his seat. "Does this place have a name?"

"Mario's. It's in the Avenues."

"You're going to have to help me out on that. Where are the Avenues?" He settled back in his seat, put the car in drive and started out.

Camille laughed softly and directed him to the restaurant. Mario's lay in a whole area of town he'd not explored yet. Higher end restaurants and shops lit up the evening street with bright lights and large windows. Big band music played softly from speakers positioned throughout the area adding to the ambiance of the already enticing

Avenues. It was a part of Blakely he hadn't even known existed.

"Do you come up here often? This is a really nice area."

"Oh, no. I can't afford to shop here, but once in a while I come up and admire the dresses in the windows. It's a great place to spend your Christmas cash, if you save it for a couple years." She giggled.

They pulled up in front of the restaurant and a valet hurried to the car. He opened Camille's door and helped her to the sidewalk. Tope had already exited the car when the valet came around to the driver's side. He dropped the keys into the young man's hand. The valet handed him a numbered ticket, which Tope dropped into his pocket, then hurried around the car to his date.

Camille smiled and took his arm. They strolled together into the restaurant and waited to be seated.

Tope looked around nervously. "I feel under dressed and unscheduled. Maybe we should've made a reservation."

"Check out the dining room. It only sounds fancy, but it's mainly expensive. No one dresses up to go to dinner in Blakely, and the only time you need a reservation at Mario's is on a Saturday night, if you come in after seven. It's more ambiance than anything up here, and a bit more spendy, but it's not New York by any stretch."

The waiter came around and directed them to their table. Camille was right. The dress was casual but the décor displayed a simple elegance. Jeans and nice shirts and blouses seemed the order of the evening. Tope slid into his chair as the waiter held Camille's chair and moved it gently into the table. He came around the side of the table and handed each of them a menu.

"Can I get you something to drink? Some wine, perhaps?"

"Would you bring us a Chianti Classico, if you have it?"

"Oh, we certainly do, sir. I'll have that right out."

As the waiter left, Tope finally relaxed and sat back in his chair. Who was this beauty sitting across the table from him? He decided to find out.

"I know nothing about you. Are you originally from Blakely?"

"Born and raised. We had a cattle ranch just outside of Blakely for many years. I grew up on the ranch and when my parents died I sold it. That's how I bought my house. Paid cash so I wouldn't have to worry about losing it if the job market went south." Her voice softened as the sentence ended.

"I take it you and Tug were close?"

"I don't know if you would call us close, really. He was my boss and I was his Administrative Assistant. You work with someone like that and you learn to anticipate their needs, you know what they're going to ask you for next and you have it ready. It's kind of a unique arrangement. He was kind and pleasant to work for."

Changing the subject, Tope decided to go back to the topic of her family. "Did you have brothers or sisters?"

Camille sighed and smiled. "No, it was just me. When my parents died, my dad's last words to me were concern that I was being left all alone. He told me he would always be with me and that I'd hear him whisper in my ear." She smiled and a light rosy blush grew, covering her cheeks. "Sometimes I think I really do hear him." She paused a moment and looked up at him, scanning his face in a way that made his stomach lurch. "How about you? What's your story?"

"Pretty much the same as you, except my parents are both still living. They are in the D.C. area. I have no siblings, either. Something happened when I was born and my mother was unable to have any more children. They thought maybe they'd adopt, but I guess they never got around to it. Did you go away to college after high school?"

"Kind of, but I came back after the first semester. I missed my family and I missed the ranch. I thought I'd go back at some point and get my degree in Veterinary Medicine, but so far I've not done that. I can't even tell you why. I've taken a lot of online courses, but there are many classes I need that I have to be in a classroom setting to accomplish. So, I keep taking what I can and one day I'll finish it up."

"I'm sure you'd be wonderful at that, especially having grown up on a ranch."

The waiter returned with the wine and poured each of them a glass, setting the remaining bottle in ice. Camille sipped hers thoughtfully and their conversation lulled.

"You're thinking awfully hard over there." Tope watched her face grow pensive. "Anything I can help with?"

She set her goblet down softly and put her chin in her hands. "What is Tope short for?"

Tope smiled and gently swirled his wine in the goblet. He leaned into the table. "Actually, nothing. My parents went to school in Topeka and liked the town so much they named me after it, shortening the name to Tope. Nothing real special about it, except a good memory for them."

"Where did you come from? Are you planning on staying?"

Tope was suddenly aware he'd need a cover story, and it needed to be solid. He forced himself to speak carefully so his story would stay the same with each telling hereafter. "I grew up in Wisconsin. My dad worked there as an accountant and my mother taught piano."

"That sounds nice. What's Wisconsin like?"

"Very cold in the winter, summers are nice with lots of lakes to swim in, lots of great places to go camping. We camped a lot when I was growing up, and I always took a friend with me when we went."

Tope wasn't exactly lying. They had camped in Wisconsin as a kid and he really did take a friend along. His dad really was an accountant and his mother did teach piano, but all that took place in D.C., not Wisconsin.

"You moved here from Wisconsin, then?"

"Yeah, I did, kind of glad to get away from those cold winters. Police work up there will freeze you solid and all the worst crimes seem to happen in the winter for some reason." Tope needed to change the subject and fast. He had no idea how much crime happened in Wisconsin and where.

"When did you begin working for Tug?"

Camille pulled her napkin off the table and set it carefully in her lap, running her hands over it several times to smooth out the folds. "I, uh, I don't actually remember. He didn't open his detective agency until he came back from Iraq, and I didn't know him before. He posted a help wanted ad and I answered it. I don't really remember when that was."

"You don't know how long you've worked for him?"

"No, no I really don't."

Tope was fast becoming very interested in the turn the conversation was taking. The waiter returned to take their order, but they'd really not even looked at their menus.

"I'm sorry, can you come back? We're not quite ready."

"Certainly sir. I'll be back in a few minutes."

Camille had already picked up her menu and appeared to be hiding behind it. He picked his up and began scanning the pages, not sure what had just happened. *She can't even make a* guess *about how long she's worked for this guy? That makes no sense. Why would that possibly be a big secret?* He settled on lasagna, mostly because he wanted to finish their conversation, but he wasn't even sure how he'd ever get back to it. The waiter, seeing they'd laid they're menus on the table, returned for the order.

"What will the lady be ordering tonight?" he asked her politely.

"I'll have the lasagna with Italian dressing on the salad."

The waiter turned to Tope. "And for you, sir?"

"I'll have the same, but Thousand Island on the salad."

"Very good. We'll have that out in a minute."

Tope thanked him and once the waiter was out of earshot, he leaned into the table.

"You know we're in the middle of a murder investigation, right? And when you tell me you have no idea how long you worked for the man who was murdered, that makes me feel like there's something you're not telling me. You needn't be worried about telling me anything, Camille. This is what I do for a living."

Camille's face suddenly drained of color. She looked down at the table, fiddled with the fork, then dropped her hands into her lap.

"I...I'm not sure I'm hungry. Maybe we should go." She started to stand and he reached across the table and covered her hand with his.

"Don't go. Besides, I'm your ride home, and I really want to try this lasagna."

She smiled faintly and remained in her seat, looking at anything but the man on the other side of the table. Tope had hit a wall for sure. *Why didn't she just throw out a number? Is she a lousy liar? Any number would have worked, unless we decide to look into her background. Maybe we should do that anyway.*

"Camille." His voice was soft; his hand still covered hers. "I'm right here. Look at me."

It seemed as if it would take a very large pair of solid steel pliers to turn her head back to the table, but she finally stared blankly at him for what seemed like several minutes. When she spoke, he couldn't believe what he was hearing.

"It's my fault Tug is dead. He was protecting me, and he died protecting me. It's my fault."

Tope had to wonder, at this point, if there were any *other* women who thought Tug Carlson's death was their fault.

Chapter Eleven

Camille's large eyes filled with tears and spilled over, running down her face. She bowed her head, allowing her thick dark hair to hide the pain now so apparent on her face.

Tope flagged down the waiter and paid for the wine, giving him a generous tip. "Please cancel the food order. Here is a little extra for your trouble. Thanks."

The couple left the restaurant with Tope's arm around Camille's waist, holding her up and helping her to the car.

By the time the valet service brought the car around and Tope slid into the driver's seat, Camille had calmed down and was better able to speak. The words flew unprompted from her mouth.

"My father, Herbert Cofford, was a spy during World War II. I didn't know this until I was going through his things and I found two documents that seemed to go together. One was in some kind of cypher, and looking closely at the other one, it appeared it was the key to decrypt the cypher. I had no idea what they were and I didn't really care. It was just junk to me."

Camille dabbed her eyes and Tope put his arm around her shoulders and pulled her closer beside him. She laid her head on his shoulder and the tears began rolling down her face much faster than before.

"I don't really know what happened, or how any news of the documents ever got out, but all of a sudden this large man showed up at my door and asked to speak to my father. I told him my father had passed away several weeks prior, but he wouldn't stop coming back and asking to go through my father's things. He said there was something my father had that belonged to him. He became consistently more aggressive, sometimes holding the door open when I tried to close it. He said his name was Clyde Naples, but I don't think that was his real name."

"He got more and more insistent as time went by and I stopped opening the door to him. I finally told Tug about him and Tug said he'd take care of it. Within a matter of days, Tug was dead. I'd given him the documents and he said he'd keep them safe for me. I don't know what was on them, but Tug thought he might. He never told me what he thought was there, he was very quiet about it and just said it was good to have them somewhere safe. He told me it was very dangerous to have the documents in my possession because there were obviously people out there who were looking for them. He said if there was one guy looking for them, there would be more."

Tope could see the more she spoke, the faster the words came and he was certain she would begin to hyperventilate if she didn't slow down. He was certain, from the look on her face, she was becoming more agitated with each word that left her mouth.

"Okay, let's take a break here." He pulled his arm from around her shoulders and began, slowly. "First, you need to understand you're safe now. I'm going to have Sawyer meet us at the station and we'll get this figured out. But for now, you're safe. Second, we're just going to have to try this dinner thing again, for obvious reasons."

Camille looked up at him with soft, defenseless, blue eyes, searching his face, reaching into his soul; he was certain he would explode if she didn't stop. She slowly, haltingly, brought her lips to his and when they touched his heart nearly leaped out of his chest. He was certain she could feel it beating out of control. He pulled her as close to him as he could get and when she released his mouth he wondered if he'd ever be the same again. *What was that feeling?* He'd never felt like this before, never had a kiss shake him like this.

"Okay," said Tope, taking a deep breath and bringing himself back to the present. "I'm going to call Sawyer now. We'll figure this out one step at a time."

Camille smiled at him again and kissed his cheek. "Thank you," she said and then leaned back in her seat and closed her eyes. Tope knew she'd been through a lot in the last couple weeks, he knew she was going to need some time, and obviously, some rest. He wondered if she'd been getting enough sleep. Fear can prevent sleep, and she'd probably been more fearful since Tug's death. Tug was supposed to have been protecting her.

Tope had a few burning questions floating around in his head as he drove to the station. How did this man, obviously the same man who'd shot Liza, find out about these documents? Who was this guy? What was his involvement? How did he find out that Camille had given the documents to Tug, unless Tug told him and then cautioned him to back off? Whatever had happened, whatever Tug had done, it got him killed, cleanly, professionally. *Who was Clyde Naples?*

❖❖❖

They met that night with Sawyer at the station. Tope was well aware that what Camille had told him put her squarely in the center of the investigation. With difficulty, he also knew his feelings for her had to be tucked carefully away in order for him to keep a clear perspective on the case. He was going to have to figure out how to make that happen.

Still, he'd kissed a lot of women in his life, and never had he experienced what he had when Camille kissed him. It was like he'd totally forgotten who he was or why he was in Blakely. No one felt like that after one kiss. It was impossible. *Wasn't it?*

As he justified his need for control, he could feel their encounter sliding into the back of his mind, filing itself safely away for another time. When he looked at her, he wondered if she was feeling the same things. However, from the look of things, that kiss was the last thing on her mind.

Her demeanor had changed; she was in control and speaking clearly and evenly to his partner.

She watched Sawyer intently, explaining to him every detail she'd told Tope in the car only a few minutes before. Every detail. Every nuance. It was as if she'd memorized the story, and he found that very…interesting.

What is she hiding? Why the perfectly manicured story, the sudden burst of confidence? Who was this woman?

"Tope? Are you with us Tope?" Sawyer was trying to get his attention, but he was so deep in thought he'd not heard him.

"Yeah, yeah, I'm here. Sorry, got lost somewhere in my own head." He forced a smile, trying not to look at Camille. "What was the question?"

"No question," smiled Sawyer. "I was just saying you should take Ms. Cofford home. She is your date, is she not?

"Right, yes." Caught completely off guard, Tope faked a smile and walked to Camille's chair, offering her a hand up. The touch of her hand brought their kiss racing back to the front of his brain. *Stop being such a girl.*

"I'll just, you know, I'll just take her home now. Because…it was a date, and now it's not, I mean, it is, it's just, well, over…now, right?"

Sawyer looked at him like his face was melting. "Are you alright?"

Tope rolled his eyes, trying to let Sawyer know what a ridiculous question that was, at the same time feeling totally ridiculous.

"After you drop her off, why don't you come back here and we'll go over some things."

Tope nodded as he and Camille left the room.

"I'm sorry if I've upset you," she began. "I didn't mean to, but once you asked me about Tug, I kind of fell apart."

Even in the dim lights of the dash, Tope could see the stress had returned. Was she playing him? How could she know what he was thinking? She was all confidence and show with Sawyer, but when she was alone with him, she's suddenly demure and defenseless. He was being played, and he could play along.

"Don't worry about it, Camille. I think it's safe to say you've been through a lot."

Camille stared out the window. Tope would have paid good money to know what she was thinking. He hated the fact that he was so taken with her, so infatuated. That was it. It was just infatuation, heat of the moment, danger, her need for protection…certainly all these things factored into his desire to protect her.

Watching her talk to Sawyer helped him see things more clearly, in a really murky, not easy to see kind of way. *If one more thing that's half-truth and confusion is thrown into this pot of stew, I swear I'll go back to D.C. and take my chances with the mob. This case gets more and more insane each day.*

Tope pulled up to the front of Camille's home. Camille unlatched her seatbelt, then gazed at him with those beautiful blue eyes. "I suppose we should call it a night." She looked at him questioningly.

"Yeah, I suppose. But once this investigation is over, we're going to redo this date.

Agreed?" He wasn't about to let her suspect he was on to her.

"Agreed."

Tope exited the car and came around to the passenger side, helping Camille onto the sidewalk. They walked in silence up to the door and as she stuck the key in the lock, Tope spoke.

"I had a great time, what little time we had. But, Camille, if we're going to find who killed Tug, you're going to have to level with me. If my being involved with you outside the office will interfere with your ability to trust me and tell me the truth, then we will need to end this now. You're hiding things. You know it and I know it. When you're ready, I hope you'll tell me what it is you seem to be unable to share. You have my number. When you're ready, call me."

Camille stiffened visibly. Staring at the door she raised her chin and he thought she might comment on what he'd said, but she said nothing. Without looking at him Camille turned the key and the door opened. Tope wanted to reach out for her, stop her, kiss her again and hope she would open up more. His feelings assumed her innocence, but his brain questioned every move she made. She walked inside and softly closed the door.

Tope turned, stepped off the porch, and onto the paved walk. A flood of feelings overpowered him. His emotions wanted to return to the kiss, remember it, feel it again, but his brain was having none of it. It took every ounce of strength he had to swallow the desire he felt for this woman. Even with his suspicions, his heart wanted more.

He got in the car, pulled away from the curb, and returned to the station.

Chapter Twelve

When Tope arrived back at Sawyer's office, Sawyer was already working on the board. He'd written "Tug Carlson's Murder" across the top of it with a horizontal line underneath going to the left and the right. Off of the horizontal line he drew short vertical lines straight down and at the end of each vertical line wrote the names of all the players in the crime so far. It looked like a macabre page of genealogy. Sawyer turned when Tope entered.

"Here's the diagram of the crime, as I see it," said Sawyer, waving his hand with the black marker still in it, across the board. Pointing to each item he'd written he continued.

"We have the shooter, the man who killed Tug Carlson. We have the explosion and subsequent theft of the item in Tug's safe deposit box. Then there's Liza, the man who shot her, Camille and the document we took from Tug's office. Anything I'm missing?"

"Wait. Before you start that, I need to share an observation." Sawyer turned to face Tope, and

Tope continued. "I need you to know the story Camille told you was the *exact* same story she told me. Not similar to the one I heard, but word for word the same. It was memorized, and I find that a bit suspicious."

Sawyer studied his partner. "I appreciate you telling me that. You didn't have to, and I know you care for Camille. You're going to need to tread very carefully, Tope; I know that you know that. She's going to have to be ruled out as a suspect, and you'll need to put a hold on the relationship until we can determine her involvement, if there is any."

Tope nodded, walked to the board and picked up the marker. He drew another line down from the main line, next to Camille. "We have Camille's father, and we have the same man who shot Liza knocking on Camille's door demanding the documents her father had."

"Why would Camille's father be any part of this? Didn't he die years ago?" Sawyer stared at the board, puzzled.

Tope studied the board. "Yes, but remember what she said? She said she was going through his things and found both documents. Where would he get his hands on documents like this? Why would he hold onto them in an old box in the attic of his home?"

Sawyer stared at the words on the board. "A quick search of the Military Archives will tell us more about Mr. Cofford, I believe. We should start there. Maybe if we find out who he was and what he knew it will tie all these pieces together."

Sawyer sat down at his desk, ready to begin a database search. Tope tapped his shoulder. "I'd be willing to bet I have a higher government clearance than you do, and will get more information. Not bragging or anything. Just sayin'."

Sawyer chuckled and stood. "Right, but a word of caution. Once you put a password in there, and someone sees that it's yours, it won't be hard to trace back to this computer in a matter of seconds."

Tope put his hand firmly on Sawyer's shoulder and forced him back down into his chair. "Well put. I'll take your wisdom over my clearance level any day of the week. Knock yourself out."

Sawyer chuckled again and turned to his computer, logging into the Government and Military database. They searched for several minutes, until they came to the conclusion they'd found the right man. They found Herbert Cofford, but he was from New York City, and died at the Battle of the Bulge at the age of nineteen.

"There has to be some mistake. Maybe her father's records didn't get put into the database. Maybe they missed him and there were actually two Herbert Coffords." Sawyer was grasping at anything that might make some sense.

"I don't think so."

Sawyer entered a different site and found Herbert Cofford of Blakely, Iowa. "This Herbert Cofford had the same Social Security Number as Herbert Cofford of New York. He had the same Military ID, but was years younger. It sure looks to me like Camille's father was living under a stolen identity, unless he was Herbert Cofford II."

Tope stared at the screen, hoping if he stared hard enough the data would change to be something more to his liking. It didn't happen. "Do you think she knows this? Do you think she's not really Camille Cofford?"

"There's only one way to know for sure. We need to talk to her."

Sawyer was already standing and reaching for his jacket. "Even if we have to get her out of bed, we need to know what she knows and what she doesn't know."

In minutes they were in Sawyer's car and on their way to Camille's home. "Do you think he actually did serve in the military? Under a real name and changed it after he was released from duty?" Sawyer couldn't seem to stop asking questions that had no answers.

"I can't think of a reason anyone would do that. Possibly he was part of a deep cover operation back then, but why would Tug think the documents Camille gave him were important enough to store in two separate places? It was World War II." Tope and Sawyer came to the same conclusion.

"Maybe he didn't serve in World War II." They both said it at the same time, both of them staring out the front window.

Tope shook himself to clear his mind. "Okay, this is getting too deep. I'm sure there's a perfectly logical explanation for this. We need more facts and less guessing. Let's just see what Camille says."

Tope directed Sawyer to her home; the lights were on. It was only 10 pm by this time and she was obviously still up. They went to the front door and heard footsteps, immediately followed by the sound of something or someone being thrown around the room, followed by the sound of breaking glass and the loud crashing noise of furniture being shoved out of the way and overturned.

Tope and Sawyer drew their guns and Tope took hold of the doorknob and turned it silently. Once inside they found Camille semi-conscious on the floor of the living room with a man standing over her; the room was in complete disarray.

Sawyer called out "BPD, stop right there!" The intruder took off running with Sawyer right behind him heading toward the back of the home.

"Camille? Camille?" Tope knelt beside her, hoping for a response. She was breathing softly and bleeding badly from a cut on her forehead. He pulled a doily off of an end table that had lost its lamp in the struggle. As gently as he could, he placed it over the cut and held it firm. Camille moaned softly and her eyes fluttered open and then closed again.

"Did…you…is he…still…?" Her eyes remained closed. "Head…hurts."

"Sawyer's after him, but he's not in the house now. Lay still, I'm calling an ambulance."

He pulled his phone from his jacket pocket with his free hand and dialed 911. In moments the ambulance sped up the street, stopping in front of the house. Paramedics came in and began working on Camille. Tope stepped back to get out of their way. "Holler at me when you're ready to leave." The paramedic nodded and Tope went in search of Sawyer.

Sawyer wasn't in the house and keeping his gun out, Tope found the switch just inside the back door and turned on the patio lights. Sawyer lay unconscious in the grass just off the patio.

"Hey! Got another victim out here!" He called to the EMTs and two of them hurried to Tope, now kneeling beside his partner.

"Step back, please," said the first EMT out the back door. Sawyer was beginning to come around and was bleeding lightly from a wound on his left upper arm.

"I'm fine, it's just a scratch. I must have hit my head when I fell. I'm fine. Just need a minute to get my bearings." Sawyer was struggling to sit up.

The EMTs were checking his eyes and the bump forming on the back of his head. "Please lie still, sir, we need to make sure you're not injured anywhere else."

"I'm fine really…"

Tope could see Sawyer either wasn't seriously injured, or was simply just being stubborn. Either way, he returned to the living room to see how Camille was doing. She'd been loaded onto a gurney and was on her way out to the waiting ambulance.

"She may need some stitches, and possibly a slight concussion, but she should be alright. We're taking her to the hospital to get her checked out. I doubt they'll keep her overnight, so she may need a ride home once they're done."

"I'll be over there in a few minutes. Thanks, guys." Tope nodded to the two men and returned to his partner. Sawyer was standing and an EMT was trying to convince him a doctor should have a look at him. He was refusing the offer adamantly, holding an icepack on the back of his head given him by the tech who was tending him.

"I'll keep an eye on him. The ambulance is ready to go." Tope shot a flat stare at Sawyer. "He's a bit stubborn." The tech nodded and went through the house and out to the waiting ambulance. The ambulance left amidst flashing lights and screaming siren.

"What happened?" Tope was going back into the house to check it and lock it up.

"He was waiting for me when I came through the back door. He had a knife and cut up my best shirt. I should have arrested him for that alone." Sawyer scowled at the slice through his shirt sleeve.

"Yes, well, things don't always work out the way we want, now, do they?"

"He must have hit me with the knife handle and knocked me out."

"Scared you, did it?" Tope was smiling smugly.

"Oh, yes, that's it," said Sawyer following him back into the house. "Yes, I was so scared I passed out." His voice was thick with sarcasm. "Would a tiny bit of sympathy be so hard? It hurts, you know."

"Well, you did let him get away."

Sawyer shoved Tope's shoulder and laughed softly. "Stop being a jerk or I'll take you off the case."

"I'll tell Amerson. He likes me best."

Sawyer scoffed, otherwise ignoring the comment. "What did you find out from Camille?"

He was gazing around the room. "She had to be putting up a pretty good fight for several minutes before we got here. How does an administrative assistant fight off an attacker twice her size?"

Tope scanned the room before going to the front door and switching off the light. "She was pretty out of it when she came to, so we'll have to get details later. And there are self-defense courses people take, you know. Maybe she's a black belt in Karate."

"Yeah, and maybe I'm a fabulous baker. Well, actually, I *am* a pretty fabulous baker. Sawyer laughed lightly and headed to the door. "Let's get to the hospital." Tope was chuckling at his partner and followed him out to the car.

"You're not driving, you know, so hand over the keys."

Sawyer would have argued if his head didn't hurt so bad. He reached into his pocket with his free hand and tossed the keys to Tope. "Don't hit any bumps. I have a headache."

The attending physician allowed one of the detectives into the exam room on the condition no questions were asked about the attack. He stressed that Camille needed to rest. Tope went in and Sawyer took a seat in the waiting room.

Camille smiled softly when Tope came through the door.

"How are you feeling?" He asked as he sat down on the edge of the bed.

"A little dizzy. The doctor said he might need to keep me overnight for observation if it doesn't go away in a little while. I'm so glad you came back. I don't know what I would have done if you hadn't. Why *did* you come back?"

"We can talk about that later. Right now, you just need to rest. I have to get Sawyer home to his family, but if you need me, just give me a call. I can take you home if they decide to let you go tonight."

"It's awful late. In fact," she glanced up at the clock. "It's 12:30 in the morning, which means it's already tomorrow. I'm sure I'll be staying."

"Let me know. If I don't hear from you, I'll talk with you tomorrow."

Tope left the room and went out to the waiting area, where he found Sawyer waiting patiently with the icepack still on his head. Sawyer had already called Esley and let her know where he was. He dropped Tope at the station so he could get his car and then headed home.

Tope arrived at his hotel, thinking it might be time to get an apartment. It was clear he was going to be here for the long haul. No mini vacations driving around in his down time to see the area and surrounding states as he'd planned. Although with spring still in the air, it didn't seem like such a bad place to be. The nights were balmy, the days were sunny and beautiful, not to mention the scenery. He smiled as he walked into the hotel. That scenery had a lot to do with Camille.

Arriving at his room, he turned the key in the door, switched on the entry hall light, and dropped his keys in the glass bowl he kept on the stand by the door. He took his revolver from the holster and laid it on the table next to the keys. He removed his coat and walked into the separate living room, blindly dropping it onto the sofa. A voice called from the darkness before he had a chance to switch on the living room light.

"I know who you are."

Chapter Thirteen

Tope's mind raced, wondering who could possibly have found out where he was and what he was doing. He calmly reached over, turned on the light, and found a vaguely familiar stranger sitting comfortably in the easy chair, staring at his hands in his lap.

"Yeah? That's interesting, because I know who I am as well. Funny how that works." He peered steadily at the man in the chair, forcing a calm demeanor. "Maybe you could tell me who *you* are and what you're doing in my hotel room."

When the man looked up, Tope recognized him right away. This was the man who'd put both Liza and Camille in the hospital.

"Oh, wait," said Tope, his voice thick with dry sarcasm. "I remember you. You're the guy who likes to attack women, with a gun and then with a fist. Yeah, I recognize you. You're not a very nice man." Tope's first impulse was to run for his gun. However, he'd learned he could get more information if he remained calm, and patient.

"My general disposition is not necessarily important. What I know about you, however, could be very important. I know you're FBI, and I know you're hiding from the D.C. mob. I'm guessing they'd really like to know where you are, since you're the one who ratted out their family. *That* wasn't very nice."

"I don't know what you're talking about. What I am is a detective with the Blakely Police Department, and unless you can give me a good reason not to, I'm going to arrest you for two counts of attempted murder and one count of criminal trespass."

The man stood nonchalantly and stretched, his hands coming within a foot or two of the ceiling. "That won't be necessary. I'm not going to turn you over to the mob; I don't work for them. However, I *do* work for an organization that would like to have something returned that was stolen from them many years ago. Something I believe very strongly you have in your possession."

"Then you believe wrong. Who are you and who are you working for?"

The man stood and strolled casually to where Tope stood. With one swift movement he brought his hand from his pocket and sprayed something into Tope's face. The intruder's image fogged and the room went black.

Tope wasn't conscious when he landed in a heap on the floor of his hotel room. He didn't see the man smile, nor hear the chuckle that escaped his lips as he ransacked the room, using a pocketknife to rip sofa cushions and the bedroom mattress apart. He also didn't witness the man angrily pulling clothes from the closet or throwing toiletries on the floor in the bathroom as he checked for hidden compartments. Tope didn't see him stride angrily to the door, slamming it behind him as he left the room. Tope didn't hear anything for several hours.

❖❖❖

When Sawyer arrived at the station the next morning, Tope wasn't there. That wasn't necessarily a bad thing, or a strange thing; but it felt bad and it felt strange. Sawyer's gut was telling him something wasn't right.

He rang Tope's cell and there was no answer. He called the hotel main desk and had them ring Tope's room, still no answer. Sawyer thought he could be on his way, but then he would've answered his cell.

"Maxwell, Farwood." Sawyer pointed to two patrolmen. "Grab a cruiser and follow me. We're going to the Hampton Hotel."

Sawyer raced to the Hampton, sure something had gone wrong. He had the clerk at the desk let him and the officers into the room where they found Tope unconscious on the floor.

"Call an ambulance!" Sawyer knelt down beside Tope and his stomach twisted. "I won't lose two of you, I just will not." He checked to see if Tope was breathing, and he was, steadily, as if he were sleeping. He checked for a wound, but there was none, and no blood. Sawyer checked Tope's head for a bump or bruise. Nothing.

"Tope. Tope. Can you hear me?" Sawyer shook his partner. He patted his face gently, trying in vain to get some reaction from him.

The two officers surveyed the room that lay in ruins around them. Sawyer scanned the room then continued checking out Tope. He pulled up his partners shirt sleeves; inspected Tope's neck, checking for needle marks on both neck and arms, but there was nothing. "I can't find a thing wrong with him. I'd think he'd been poisoned, but his breathing is steady and he appears unhurt. What happened to him? Why won't he wake up?"

The EMTs raced into the room with a gurney and began working on Tope. This ambulance calling was getting to be a regular part of Sawyer's day. He watched the paramedics, feeling almost as helpless as he had when he found Jack. There were differences in the two crime scenes. Vast differences. Jack wasn't breathing. Jack was gone. His stomach wrenched again at the thought.

"He'll be okay?"

"All we know is he's breathing, and that's always a good thing. We'll get him to the hospital and the doctors will take over from there."

Tope's limp body was placed on the gurney and hurried to the elevator. Sawyer directed one of the officers to call for a CSI team. While he waited for their arrival, he slipped into exam gloves and slowly examined the room, trying to focus on the total picture and not worry about his partner. Tope's attacker had been looking for something. There wasn't so much as a coffee cup where it should be. The room had been destroyed. The entry, however, appeared to be left untouched.

Tope's car keys were in a bowl on a small table there, along with his gun. The two officers checked the rooms to make sure they were clear and returned to where Sawyer was reviewing possible scenarios.

"If he put his gun down here, and car keys in this bowl," Sawyer pointed to the entry table, "he suspected nothing. Either he let the perp in, or he was already inside when Tope arrived and possibly in the living room, or maybe the bathroom. Could have snuck up from behind." He continued scanning the room, standing in the center of it and inspecting every inch. Was some of this caused by a struggle? To him it looked like someone was looking for something, not like a fight had occurred. Was Tope already unconscious when the room was searched?

Clayton Hillstrom entered with his team of CSIs. "Anything interesting I need to know?" He waited for Sawyer to answer.

"This one's a puzzle. As near as I can tell Tope was poisoned; but there's no evidence of it. They'll check for needle marks when they get him to the hospital, I'm sure, but I'm wondering about something airborne. What do you think?"

Clayton watched his team methodically going about their work. "We'll see what we can find. I'll let you know if anything turns up."

"Thanks, Clayton. I'll wait to hear from you."

Sawyer's next stop would be the hospital. He needed to know what happened to Tope and how he was doing. When he arrived there, Tope was conscious, sitting up and looking a little groggy. When he saw Sawyer, he told him what had happened in his hotel room. He remembered every detail, which told both him and Sawyer that whatever was used to drug him hadn't messed with his memory.

"Whoever this guy is, he knows who I am and why I'm in Blakely. He knew I'm FBI, he even mentioned the op I was working on when my cover was blown."

Sawyer's brow furrowed and he looked down, thinking. "I'll let Captain Amerson know right away and we'll get this figured out. You got a good look at this guy's face, so we'll have you look at some mug shots - most wanted, you know the drill. We'll see if anything comes up. I've already lost one partner; I'm not planning on losing another one. We'll find this guy, and we'll find out what his game is."

"Thanks, Sawyer." The look of concern on Tope's face didn't match his words. He was worried. You don't mess with the mob, and that's exactly what he'd done. "I think they want to watch me for a while to make sure the stuff he sprayed me with isn't going to do anything other than knock me out. They're not sure what it was yet. I'll give you a call when they let me out of here."

"You have a guard at the door, so don't worry about anything. Just relax and let the doctors do what they need to do. I'll plan on checking with you tomorrow. I'm going to go have a chat with the captain now."

Sawyer rose and strode to the door.
"Hey, Sawyer?"
He turned to face his partner. "Yeah?"
"Thanks."

Sawyer grinned and left the room, heading back down to his car. He sat in the car, not moving for a few minutes, reviewing the day, but mostly reviewing his new partner. Tope even sounded like Jack, and sometimes that brought a feeling to his gut that he'd thought was long gone. Tope was a good man, every bit as good as Jack was. The fact that he looked like Jack's nearly identical twin didn't help Sawyer's insides at all. If he'd been hard to work with, it would almost have made the partnership easier. It would be easier to dislike the guy. As it was, he slipped right into Jack's position like a hand into a well-worn glove. It was uncanny.

Sawyer placed the key in the ignition and sat back again, releasing his hold on the key and dropping his hands into his lap. *Jack? Are you sending me gifts? First you save Esley, then direct me where to find her. Now you send Tope to work with me. He's so much like you. Was this really your doing?*

He smiled a wry smile and shook his head as he leaned forward and started the car.

"*You're something else, Jack. You're really something else.*"

❖❖❖

Chase Amerson was the kind of man who would drop everything when his officers needed him, and this night was no different. He'd received a call from Sawyer Kingsley telling him they needed to talk right away. It was late when he turned the key at the station and went upstairs to his office. Minutes later, Sawyer arrived and plopped down in the chair in front of the captain's desk.

"The guy who attacked Tope, possibly the same man who attacked Liza and Camille, told Tope he knew he was FBI and he knew the D.C. mob was looking for him."

"Who *is* this guy?"

"I wish I knew, but he stays very well hidden. With all the eyes out there looking for him, I can't believe we don't have a lead on him…*something*…even a bite. But we've got nothing. The guy is apparently invisible unless he wants you to see him."

"If I even had a sketch of the guy I'd run it through the database, but I don't have a thing. If Tope, Liza, and Camille can sit down with our sketch artist, then maybe, between the three of them, we can get something that would let us do a decent search."

"I've got two uniforms at Tope's door until he's released, so he's probably safe there. I don't think this perp likes to attack in public, as he has only attacked in private residences. He's very careful about who sees him, but interestingly, he makes no effort to hide his face when he's on the attack, and like any perp who's worth anything, he always wear gloves. We haven't found a single fingerprint at any of the crime scenes. Hopefully we'll be able to get a viable description from these three separate attacks."

It was late by this time and both men were feeling their fatigue. Sawyer stood and stretched. "Esley's going to forget what I look like; even worse, she'll forget my favorite meals if I don't start spending some time at home."

Captain Amerson smiled. "Heaven help her if she has to get used to *that* mug twice. I'm sure once was hard enough for her."

"Funny. If I weren't so tired I'd punch you, if you weren't my captain."

Amerson chuckled. "Kind of sounds like that old saying, 'If we had some bacon we could have bacon and eggs, if we had some eggs.'"

"You lost me. I'm going home."

❖❖❖

Sawyer arrived at the station the next morning feeling like it'd already been a long day, when in reality it had only just begun. He hadn't slept well, which contributed a great deal to his feeling of exhaustion.

His first stop was the lab, where they'd been working on the dart from Tug's desk at his apartment. Also, he needed to make sure the DNA results for the case he was on prior to Tope's arrival had been transferred to the newly assigned detectives. There'd been no time for follow up on the old case with all that was happening in his current assignment.

Joe Branoff was working the counter when Sawyer entered the Lab. "Hey Joe, how's it going?"

"It's going," he said with a smile, reaching across the counter to shake Sawyer's hand. "You've been a bit busy, I see. Where should we start?"

"Well, first, did the DNA from the Frederick's investigation get to the new detective on that case?"

"It did."

"Good. Just wanted to make sure. How about that dart? Have you figured out what the poison was yet?"

"Yes we did, and it was tetrodotoxin. I was going to call you on that, so I'm glad you stopped by. Tetrodotoxin comes from the puffer fish and is fairly hard to come by in these parts. I'm kind of surprised someone from Blakely would have access to it. The results of tetrodotoxin poisoning are nearly always death, and a horrible death as well."

Sawyer tapped his fingers on the counter, thinking. "We have no idea who Tug Carlson really is and what his connections are. Apparently he has access to whatever he needs, but it beats me why he'd think he needed something so lethal." Sawyer paused before continuing. "Thanks, Joe. That bit of information gives me one more question for the mile long list I already have in this case."

Joe chuckled. "Glad I could help."

Sawyer's next stop was Luke Golding's office, the CSI department head. "Hey Luke," he said, coming through the door. "You got a minute?"

"Always. What's on your mind?"

"I'm sure you'd have let me know this, but I thought I'd double check with you. Did you find anything of interest in Tug Carlson's office, in his apartment or in Ja--I mean, Tope's hotel room?"

"We're all making that mistake," smiled Luke. "The likeness is a little disconcerting, you know?"

"Yeah, I do."

"As far as what we found, nothing that would knock your socks off. The usual. There was no residue on the carpet at Tope's hotel, either. I don't know what was used on him, but it dissipated without leaving a trace behind. Kind of strange."

"Yeah it is. The doctors are having the same results. They want to make sure Tope isn't going to have any after effects."

"Sorry I couldn't be more helpful."

Sawyer stood and stretched. "Not a problem. We'll get it figured out."

The detective made his way down the hall and into the bullpen, walking straight through to Captain Amerson's office.

"Any news on the document we found in Tug Carlson's filing cabinet?" Sawyer was talking as he entered and sat down in his usual chair.

"I was just sitting here chewing on that. This document adds a whole lotta questions to your investigation, which if I'm right, already has its fair share of questions."

"Yes, absolutely." Sawyer shook his head and sighed. "The hospital isn't releasing Tope until they're comfortable knowing he's not going to have any problems. They can't identify the substance used to knock him out, and neither can Forensics. Are we dealing with a whole new drug here? One we haven't seen before?"

"It sounds like it, but you've got bigger issues than that right now." Captain Amerson placed his hands; fingers laced together, over his head and rested them on his graying hair in his usual thinking pose. "I probably should have told you, but we sent that coded letter to the NSA for scrutiny, and they discovered something."

"What?"

"That it's a list of plans for now obsolete equipment from the Korean, Vietnam and Iraq wars. What they can't figure out, is what the rush is to get at this obsolete and outdated information. It makes no sense."

Chapter Fourteen

Tope woke from a short nap to see Camille holding his hand, her worried eyes focused on his face. One eye was still swollen nearly shut, and her lip was cut. She had several large bruises on her face and stitches graced the cut on her forehead.

He smiled and squeezed her hand. "Hard day at the office?" He enjoyed the feel of her skin and kept her hand in his.

She smiled softly. "What happened to you?"

"A little tussle at my hotel is all. How are you feeling? You should be home, resting."

"This looks like more than a little tussle to me. What happened?"

"You know how these things are," Tope said, staring into her eyes, "I can't really talk about it. Police business and all."

Camille knew this had something to do with her situation and it made her insides twist. It seemed everything she did caused pain to others. She continued as best she could.

"I…I just heard from Captain Amerson that you were here. I never got to thank you for saving me, but I sure didn't expect you to be in the hospital!"

He smiled at her and rubbed the back of her hand with his thumb. He knew he shouldn't be doing anything to encourage this relationship, but her eyes were so sad, so soft, and pleading. So *blue*. He was concerned for her safety, and seeing her as bruised and stitched as she was made it difficult for him to distance himself. He tried to ignore the nagging voice in the back of his head telling him to back away.

"Was your house a disaster? I'm sorry you had to go home that mess and deal with the experience all over again. You might consider changing your locks."

There had been no after effects of whatever was used on him, and however much he wanted to kick his mistrust of her to the curb, Tope knew Camille was not being honest with him or with his partner. That ever-present thought was the only thing that kept him careful; however, he wasn't being very careful at the moment, and he knew it. Her response to his suggestion completely took him by surprise and popped that mistrust into overdrive.

"I didn't go home. I've booked a room at the Hampton. I'm too frightened to stay in my house. Even changing the locks wouldn't help. I need lots of people around me, and the only place I can go to have that is either an apartment complex or a hotel. I don't want to be alone at this point."

Tope had barely listened to her once she'd said the name of the hotel. His head spun with questions, none of which he could ask her. Fortunately, only one made it out of his mouth, and it was innocent enough. "What made you choose that hotel?"

Camille cocked her head, her brow knitted. She'd obviously heard the mistrust in his voice. "What difference does it make? I just chose a hotel. Was I supposed to check with you when I made that choice?"

Before he could answer she stood and lifted her coat from the end of the bed. There was a sudden chill to her attitude as she put the coat on. Her smile never touched her eyes. "I should go. There is a lot of work to be done to shut down Tug's office."

She obviously did not want to get into a conversation about her new living arrangements. As he watched her stride stiffly out the door, Tope was sure he'd never worked on a more convoluted case in his career. Camille made his heart pound and his brain scream at him, all at the same time. He needed to get out of the hospital and back into the investigation. Tope pressed the button to call the nurse. He was being discharged one way or another.

❖❖❖

Sawyer and Captain Amerson were discussing the cypher found in Tug's strong box when Sawyer's phone rang.

The captain nodded for him to answer the call as he began leafing through some papers on his desk.

"Kingsley."

Listening to the caller, he was clearly confused.

"She said *what?*" His eyes met those of his captain. "Stay where you are, Tope, I'll be right there."

Sawyer ended the call and stared at his captain.

"I don't know what's going on, Captain, but that was Tope and he says Camille just booked a room at his hotel. Something really stinks about that."

Amerson's face softened. "It could be no more than a booked hotel room, you know. She's too scared to go home so she booked a room somewhere she would feel safe. Had Tope ever mentioned to her where he was staying?"

"I don't know, but I'm going to find out. There was something odd about his date with her, but with everything that happened that night, I never got to discuss it. I'll head down there and let you know what I find out."

"Okay, but remember, coincidences do happen."

Sawyer nodded and headed through the door.

When he arrived at the hospital, Tope was dressed and sitting on the side of his bed, ready to go.

"You're cleared for take off?"

Tope grinned. "Got my walking papers right here." He lifted the papers off the bed stand and shook them gently. "We're missing something, Sawyer. We're missing something that's hiding in plain sight."

The nursing staff came in with the traditional wheelchair.

"Really?" Tope gave the nurse a 'this is ridiculous' look and she scowled back at him.

"Really. Now get in."

Sawyer couldn't help chuckling as Tope sat down and was wheeled out. Sawyer retrieved his car and pulled it to the curb. Before he could get around to the passenger side to help Tope into the vehicle, he was already inside and putting on his seatbelt.

"That was fast," he said to the nurse. "Guess he's ready to go home."

"We'll miss that one. Like an extra left toe…" The nurse chuckled at her own joke, then said affectionately, "But we'll miss him all the same."

Sawyer laughed and walked back around the car, sliding into the driver's seat. "I get the feeling you were a bit of a pain in the butt for the nursing staff?"

Tope's face grew innocent, his eyes wide. "Whatever gave you that idea? I think that's an unfair assessment from only one nurse. You'd need to do a full survey of all the staff to have a clear picture. I know *some* of them liked me. A couple of them *really* liked me." He smiled slyly.

"Right."

Sawyer put the car in gear and started through the parking lot.

"Captain thinks Camille's hotel choice is probably just a coincidence. There isn't much to choose from in the way of nice hotels in this town."

"I have to disagree. When I tried to talk to her about it, she put on her coat and left. It was…odd."

"Women are funny, you know. You might have just hurt her feelings. You think?"

"Oh, please. That's crazy! She's either scared out of her mind or she's playing a really good game of cat and mouse. Trouble is, I'm feeling more and more like the mouse."

"I'm not doubting that part, but did you actually tell her where you were staying?"

Tope thought for a moment. "No, no it never came up."

"There. You see? You just hurt her feelings by questioning her move to the hotel."

"That's ludicrous. She's hiding something."

Sawyer chuckled and shook his head. "There's a mystery. I agree there is something she's not saying, and it does look suspicious. Okay, maybe a little more than suspicious. We'll check into it, but right now we need to get you moved into a new hotel room and settled. Once you're up to it, we'll review our board at the station and see if we can pick up where we left off, agreed?"

Tope's disgruntled look came off just like Jack's used to. It made Sawyer smile. He acted a lot like Jack, looked at things the same way Jack would have looked at them. Sawyer was beginning to hope that Tope would want to stay on as his partner even after this case was solved. If it ever was solved.

"Would you be more comfortable if we changed your hotel altogether?"

"No, there's a part of me that wants to see how this plays out. I need to find out, for my own piece of mind, if she's playing a game or seriously doesn't know I'm staying there. And I *don't* need you to babysit me, you know," he complained. "I can move my stuff all by myself. I'm *such* a big boy."

"Yeah, but it's so much more fun to make you feel like you can't. I mean, how often do I get to babysit?" Then answering his own question he said, "Okay, I get to babysit quite often, really, but I mean, babysit a grown up baby."

"Okay, that's it. You are *not* helping me. You will wait in the lobby and I'll move my own stuff."

Sawyer couldn't help laughing. It felt good to actually like his partner for a change.

When they arrived at the hotel, Tope went to the front desk to get keys to a new room and grab a cart for hauling clothes, toiletries, and suitcases from his old room to the new one. The young man at the desk couldn't have been older than twenty. His blond hair and dark eyes searched Tope, not masking his distaste for what had happened to the customer's first room.

"Oh, there's no need Mr. Daniels. We've taken care of all of that for you. Here is your new room key." The clerk's eyes narrowed as he handed the key to Tope. "We left it up to you where you want to put things, but I'm sure the new room will fit your needs."

"Really? That makes for a much more pleasant conversation with my partner over there. Thank you for doing all of that."

"It was our pleasure. I hope the remainder of your stay will be better than the last few days."

Tope got the impression the young man wouldn't have been hurt if he'd been told Tope was moving to another hotel. The clerk's disappointed look as he handed off the keys pretty much said it all.

"Enjoy your day." The sarcasm was becoming a little thick.

Tope smiled and took the keys. He and Sawyer headed to the elevator and up one floor further than his previous room. As promised, all of his things were there, complete with suitcases ready to be unpacked.

"It's so nice to be home." Tope smiled sardonically. "Truthfully, I wonder if I shouldn't work harder at finding an apartment or a house."

"You're sure welcome to stay with us until you can find a place. We have a guest room."

"No, I'd never go to work. I'd stay there and play with Jack all day. I don't know how you tear yourself away. He's a great kid."

"Live with him for about a week and you'll find the tearing away thing isn't so hard to do. Esley is a great mom. I don't know how she deals with his tantrums and his tears and keeps that happy face on."

Tope's smile faded. "I think I missed that boat. I'm too set in my ways to start a family now."

"It's never too late. You're younger than I am! Just wait until that right one comes along. You'll definitely know her when you see her. Although, truthfully I wanted to choke Esley for that first little while. She wasn't too happy with me, either. But we both got over ourselves and it worked out."

There was a lull in the conversation for a minute as Tope reflected on whether or not 'the one' was a liar and a traitor. His attitude immediately sank to new lows.

Sawyer spoke up. "Since you're already moved in, let's go get some lunch. I'm starving. I think I forgot to eat breakfast." Tope nodded and they left the room, heading back down to the car.

The diner was busy, but Sawyer's favorite booth was vacant. They sat down and ordered their lunch. Tope was sullen and silent. Sawyer knew exactly what he was thinking, but what he didn't know was how to fix the problem.

"It's plain to see you care about Camille, Tope. The problem with that appears to be that we don't know who she is. We don't know who her father was. We only know he wasn't who he said he was. You know what that means, right?"

Tope sighed heavily and rested his back against the booth, staring out the window. "I thought I cared for her, Sawyer. I really thought I did." Tope turned to study the face of his partner. "But clearly she's lying. She's lying about her work with Tug and she's lying about her father. I think she may be stalking me, which makes me wonder if the whole beating incident was staged. Is she a mercenary as well? Is she so selfish she would sell out her country for a few dollars? I can't love someone like that, Sawyer. I can't. So, no, I don't care for her."

Sawyer studied his hands, which were resting on the table, fingers laced together. "As much as you want to believe you don't care, it can't be turned on and off that easily."

"It can for me." Tope's eyes were like fire, his face stone.

Their waitress came with their food and once she walked away, Tope shoved his plate of hamburger and fries to the middle of the table.

"I guess I'm not hungry."

Chapter Fifteen

Camille stepped out of her car and nearly slammed the door behind her. If thoughts could spit, hers would be spitting out her ears.

I hate secrets. I hate having them, keeping them, spilling them. I hate secrets.

She attempted to keep a pleasant face and happy persona as she stepped through the sliding glass doors of the business office building where Tug had rented his office space. She strolled purposefully to the elevator and rode it to the third floor, still ranting inside herself.

The elevator stopped at the second floor, and Camille sighed, anxious to get to the agency office and get the rest of the work files closed out. James, from the accounting office down the hall from the detective agency, and her most ardent admirer, sauntered confidently into the elevator and checked that the button to the floor he needed had been pressed.

Turning to the object of his affection he began his attempt at 'smooth.' "You're looking wildly impressive today," he said, in his sexiest voice. Camille wanted to throw up, but she maintained her composure and acknowledged him with a brief smile before casting her eyes to the monitor, hoping one more floor wouldn't take too long. She was in luck. The elevator came to a stop and the doors slid open before she needed to comment. She smiled weakly and headed out the doors. Unfortunately, so did James.

"So, when are you going to give into my charms and have dinner with me?"

This had been going on for weeks. Was the man so dense? Did he not read the paper and know what her life had been like? At the very end of her patience, she did something she'd never done before. She took out her verbal knife and threw it at him.

"Charms? You have no charms, James, and therefore there is nothing to give in *to*. Now would you leave me alone and allow me to grieve for the death of my boss and get the office closed down?"

Undeterred, the young man kept up the phony confidence, sounding more ridiculous as he moved along. "Yes, I heard about that. How long do you think you'll need to grieve? I can wait." He raised one eyebrow like he'd just been stunningly clever.

Camille stopped at the agency door and slipped the key in the lock. Better the lock than his eyeball. "Have a good day," she said flatly. She walked into the office and slammed the door behind her.

She'd always tried to be polite with James, always tried to ward off his unwanted advances with an excuse or a quick getaway. He appeared to be totally oblivious to her hints. Camille refused to allow herself to feel guilty for finally telling him how she felt, only to have him gloss over it with his phony James Bond impression. This was going to require less tact than she ever imagined anyone could possess.

Gazing around the office, sadness overtook her once again and she could feel the tears well up in her eyes. Camille was certain Tug died protecting her secret. A secret he didn't even know she had. Who would protect her now?

After locking the door, she removed her coat and jumped into the day's work. There was much to do, and though she knew Tug wouldn't require her to close down his office, it was the one thing she could do for him. *I wonder if he knows I'm doing this. I wonder if it makes him happy.*

As she sat down at what was once her desk, she was determined to make sure she did the best job she could for Tug. He'd been good to her and had been the only one who would listen to her and take her fears seriously. *Now no one does.* Everyone thought the worst of her, at least everyone who mattered to her. There was only one person who truly mattered. And from his eyes, she could plainly see he doubted everything that came out of her mouth. Why wouldn't he? She sounded like some kind of CIA spook or something.

It just seemed if she were going to explain her situation to anyone, she would put that person in jeopardy, just as she had with Tug. She wouldn't go through that again, she couldn't. Tug had a girlfriend…he was happy. He'd had a life. Now because of her, he was dead. Just like her father had warned her.

"I know this is going to be difficult for you, my Camille, but you need to read this note, memorize it, then burn it. What I have attached to it are two pages of the utmost importance to the security of the United States. Guard them with your life. Tell no one you have them, but keep them. Keep them safe. One day, these will be the only way to clear your mother and I of any wrongdoing and keep you safe once and for all. You will know when the time is right to show them to someone. And you'll know who that someone is. Then you'll understand why the documents had to stay hidden for so long."

She thought she'd found that person when she found Tug. How long had she worked for him? Three days. When he died, she'd quickly gone into his books and destroyed any evidence of those three days. There was nothing left that would reveal the length of time she'd worked for Tug, and if anyone found out, she would for sure be the prime suspect in his murder.

Could she trust Tope? She had no idea who he was or where he'd come from. Her father taught her while in her teens how to determine if someone was lying to her. Tope was lying about where he'd come from. She was certain of it. And yet, it certainly seemed like he knew she wasn't being honest either, which she wasn't. How could he know that?

"A fine mess you've given me, Daddy. What am I supposed to do now?"

Camille had waited several weeks before going through the box of things her father had given her. She knew the documents were in there, she'd put them in there herself and kept the box in her attic. She didn't want to look at them, didn't want to deal with any of what was left of her father's secrets. He'd given her the documents, along with a box of other things she might like. Mostly pictures of her childhood, graduation from high school, her first try at shoeing a horse, all of it memories of a life with her father.

When she finally pulled the box down, the document he'd sworn her to protect lay on the top. She had no idea what she was supposed to do with it, so she put it back in the box and put the box back up in the attic. This time, she hid it, making sure it would be difficult to find, if anyone ever came looking.

Returning to the work of the day, she continued, separating out the current files and shredding the closed ones. Current files would be returned to each client, who would then pick a new agency to continue their investigation.

Most of the files included issues like cheating spouses, some neighborhood disputes that the police department didn't have time for; still others were suspected embezzling issues. There were all kinds of problems brought to the agency. Some had grounds for investigation; others were refused.

Standing at her desk, she continued going through the files when she opened one that was unfamiliar to her. The file label was odd, but there was nothing unusual about that, really, she'd only worked for him for three days. When she opened the file, there was a single folded page in it. That was certainly odd. Why have a useless file cluttering up his records?

Opening the note she began to read. Her hand flew to her mouth. She backed up and reached down for the arm of her chair, collapsing into it, never taking her eyes from the note.

"I know this is going to be difficult for you, my Camille, but you need to read this note, memorize it, then burn it..."

Her father's words rang in her ears and her hands shook. What was this note doing in Tug's personal files? He'd obviously hoped it would never be found. She stared at the file name and the meaning of it screamed from the page.

"Camford - 2006." She'd not noticed when she first glanced at the file how similar to her name the file was. Camille Cofford. Camford. But the year 2006 made no sense at all. Tug was in Iraq in 2006. Her father died in 2006. She didn't meet Tug until…until six months prior to Tug's death, when she'd sat on a park bench by herself and Tug had approached her asking if she would mind if he sat down. The conversation poured into her mind like a movie on the big screen.

"Not at all," Camille replied. "Please." She gestured to the bench and Tug sat down. "I was just leaving."

"You're looking pretty intense," he smiled, ignoring what she'd just said. He was a handsome man; older, tall, and well built with graying hair cut short, military style and intense green eyes. "Are you okay?"

Camille shrugged and smiled softly. "Sometimes I just miss my parents, that's all. I'm actually quite fine." She smiled her bravest smile and his look softened.

"I'm sorry for your loss, Miss..." He waited for her to answer.

"I really have to be going. Enjoy the bench." Camille stood to go and Tug grabbed her hand.

"Please don't go. I could use some conversation myself."

"But you don't even know me. I certainly don't know you, and I'm...I'm really not very good company today anyway."

Tug released her hand, allowing his own to fall helplessly into his lap. "I understand."

He sounded so tragically lonely. It was heart wrenching. Camille sat back down, suddenly more concerned for his grief than her own.

"I...I'm sorry. Are you okay? I can certainly listen, but I'm sure I won't be much help."

Tug stared at her and her stomach jumped. Unsure if it was telling her to run or stay put, she stayed put. Staring at his hands, he began with the Iraq War and how difficult acclimating back to civilian life had been. He'd been injured, and could now only hear out of one ear due to the explosion of a roadside bomb outside his Humvee. The Humvee had flipped several times, throwing him from the truck and exploding with the last roll. One of his buddies was still alive and trapped on the ground beneath the burning truck. He'd raced to pull him out of the rubble, but the Humvee exploded again, throwing Tug back and knocking him unconscious in the landing. When he came to, he was on a gurney heading to another truck. His friends who were in the Humvee with him were all dead.

Camille stared at him wide-eyed, unable to speak. She finally whispered, "How awful. I'm so sorry."

His steel blue eyes looked up at her with a soft strength that amazed her. He seemed so confident, so sure of himself, yet gentle. After all he'd been through, she was surprised there was any gentleness left in him.

"I'm sorry it's been difficult returning to civilian life. I'm so sorry for the loss of your friends. It must be very difficult. I can't imagine," she smiled at him. "I'm sure it will sound hollow, but thank you for your service to our country. What an honor it is to speak with you."

Tug said nothing, but turned his head away. "That's very nice of you to say."

"I...I mean it. I really do. It's just that...I...I have to get back to work. It's been very nice to meet you." She stood to go and this time he didn't try to stop her.

"Nice to meet you, as well."

The movie stopped and she was back in the office, staring at a note that she herself had burned so many years ago. Why did Tug have this note? Why did her father tell her to burn it if he knew there was another copy? *Did* he know there was another copy?

Thinking back on the last six months, it was more than curious now, how Tug would show up at different places she'd be. The grocery store, department store, movie house, tea room. He certainly hadn't seemed like the kind of guy who liked tea, and when she'd asked him about it, he'd smiled and said he was getting it for his girlfriend.

Who was he really? Trusting no one because of her father's words, she was surprised to remember she'd not even thought anything of that meeting. Blakely wasn't a huge town, she probably saw the same people everywhere she went, but since she didn't know them, it wasn't weird. However, looking back, now she wondered if Tug knew what he was doing and she didn't. Was she really that stupid? At least she was aware of Tope's lies. Tug hadn't shown any indication he was lying. She wondered if Tug was CIA or FBI or NSA or something. Obviously Tope wasn't any of those, he was just a city cop.

She looked down at the note in her hand once more. What was she going to do with this? She'd memorized it so many years ago, and still had it in her head. She often dreamt about these words. Tonight, she would burn it again, in an ashtray, and that would be the end of it.

There was a knock at the door. Thankful she'd locked it, she quickly stuffed the note into her bra and stood. "Who's there?"

The voice from the other side of the door brought a scowl.

"It's Sawyer and Tope, Camille, and we need to talk to you."

Chapter Sixteen

Camille stood and walked to the door trying to hide her dislike. Tope Daniels was the last person she needed to see right now. Still, she couldn't seem to make her heart agree with her head. She opened the door and she motioned for the two men to come in, trying to ignore Tope and his gorgeous blue eyes.

"How can I help you?" Her words were formal as the three sat down in the waiting area. "I'm sure I've told you everything I know."

Sawyer avoided glancing at Tope as he began. "We've found some information that we need to clarify with you, Camille. Can you tell me where your father was born?"

"I don't see how that's any of your business," snapped Camille. "It has nothing to do with Tug's death." That was a direct lie, and she knew it. Her palms were suddenly sweaty and her brain fought with the idea they could know anything about her father.

"Actually, it has a great deal to do with this investigation. You obtained, from your father, two documents. One was in code, the other the key to that code, which is missing. You gave them to Tug for safekeeping, and now he's dead. We've sent the one document we recovered to the NSA for transcription. The other document is still missing. Your father had both these documents in his possession. Why is that? What did he do for a living?"

Camille stared at Sawyer, speechless, but strong. "He was retired military."

"And what did he do for the military?"

"I have no idea. I was quite little when he served. When he retired, he was home for the most part and occasionally traveled with a small repair business he owned."

There was a knock at the door and a young man opened it, sticking his head in.

"Hey gorgeous! What's happening?"

"Not now, James." Camille stood, her face a mask of irritation.

James face split with his ever-ignorant grin. What's going on?"

"Oh, just some poisonous gas or something in Tugs office. These gentlemen are making sure the building isn't going to blow up."

James' eyes widened and he began slowly stepping backward. "You know…I…I just remembered I have to…to finish a…a thing in my office, now. Right now."

He turned and sprinted down the hall, around the corner and out of sight. Camille smiled in spite of the tension she felt as she closed the door.

She glanced sheepishly at the detectives. "Sorry, I couldn't resist."

"Who was *that*?" smirked Tope. "He was more nervous than a pig at a barbecue."

Some of the tension seemed to lift as Camille smiled softly and said, "Oh, him? Yeah, he's my night in shining armor." She chuckled softly, "I think that's the last I'll see of him, with any luck."

Tope couldn't help the chuckle that escaped his lips. She had a devilish side to her, and he liked it.

Sawyer struggled to hide his amusement.

"I'm sorry. Now, where were we?" Camille returned to her chair.

"You were saying he traveled for the repairs he did. Why the need to travel for a repair business?"

Camille gave him a flat stare, purposely avoiding Tope. "Look around you! This is farm and ranch land. People live miles apart from one another and when he got calls on broken down farm equipment it was usually two or three at a time. He'd go from one to the other, often spending a day or two at each place, depending on how long the repairs would take. If he needed parts he'd move on to the next farm and return to the one waiting on parts on his way home. He might be gone for days at a time, sometimes he'd be home the same night he left."

"I see." Sawyer sighed and pushed on. "Camille, I'm afraid I may have some…distressing news. Your father was not Herbert Cofford. Herbert Cofford died in World War II. We have reason to believe your father took his identity, but we have no idea why he would need to do that. Do you?"

"That's ridiculous," she spat. "You're wasting my time and I have a lot of work to do. You need to leave. Now."

Camille could feel her heart racing. She wanted to spill everything she knew, tell them all they wanted to know, but how could she trust them? How could she ever trust anyone again? The only man she'd ever trusted, other than her father, was dead. And it was her fault.

Camille stood as soon as she was sure her weak, shaking legs wouldn't land her in a heap on the floor. "I said *leave.*" She focused her whole attention on her anger to keep the tears from filling her eyes. The isolation and loneliness she'd felt since her father's death came to a head in the words of these men. They were lying. She knew they were lying. Her father was Herbert Cofford and her mother died when she was a baby. Who were these men, and what right did they have to question her father's identity, and her own for that matter?

Both Sawyer and Tope stood at the same time and strode to the door. Before exiting, Tope turned back to Camille. "You're scared to death. What are you afraid of? Do you know something you're not telling us, or is your fear based on the fact that your own name may not be Cofford?"

"*Get out!*"

Tope's angry expression broke her heart. She wanted to stop him, but what would she tell him? He turned and left with no other words, closing the door behind him. Camille rushed to the door and locked it before they could come back in. She needed to think. She needed *time* to think.

Sitting back down in her desk chair she stared at the pile of files yet to be reviewed and sorted. *My name is Camille Cofford. I had parents whose names were Cofford. My mother died when I was a baby. My father entrusted a note to me, along with two documents that he told me to keep safe. I have kept them safe. I've done everything my father asked me to do. He said I'd know who to trust when I found them, and I found Tug. I knew he would take care of the documents and protect me. I did it, didn't I? I found the one person, right? Just like daddy said I would. I did. Didn't I?*

She dropped her hands in her lap and sobbed. Camille had no idea if she was right or wrong, but the one thing her father had taught her was if you have to convince yourself you're right, you're probably wrong. Had she been wrong to trust Tug?

Her mind wandered to Tope. She felt he was a good person. He'd come back to the house just in time to save her from that awful Clyde Naples. Tope saved her and then more than likely, he'd been beaten for it. Was she the one who was causing these people harm? What if keeping these secrets killed Tope? She'd been the cause of one death, how could she live with herself if her silence killed another human being?

Camille stood, knowing she had to tell the whole story to Tope and Sawyer. If this was ever going to be over it had to be dealt with and half-truths weren't going to cut it. She was tired of running, tired of never connecting with people, tired of looking over her shoulder and never knowing why or what she was looking for.

Grabbing her coat from the coatrack she hurried out the door, locking it behind her. As she jogged down the hallway to the elevator she had no idea what she was going to say to these two men, or if they would even believe her, but she was going to tell her story. Maybe…hopefully…once and for all…she was going to be done with it. Even Tug hadn't heard the whole story. Maybe if he'd had all the information, he wouldn't have died.

The elevator doors opened and Camille stepped inside. Her mind was spinning as she struggled to find a way to explain to Tope how she'd gotten caught up in this mess. Deep in thought, she didn't hear the elevator doors open.

"Are you looking for me?"

Camille looked up and into the face of Tope Daniels. "I…I…was just thinking we should talk." She looked nervously from side to side outside the elevator to make sure no one had heard her. "Privately."

"Sawyer's in the car. We'll go down to the station. Will that be agreeable?"

She nodded her head in the affirmative and he took her by the arm and led her out to the car.

❖ ❖ ❖

Watching from behind a large plant, the man who called himself Clyde Naples frowned. He'd missed her by only minutes. He should have killed that phony cop when he had the chance. He'd found nothing in the hotel room, no sign of the document from Tug's office, and now the cops had the girl. There was information he needed from her, and he needed it fast. People were getting impatient with him.

Placing his hand in his coat pocket, he rolled the syringe around between his thumb and pointer finger. Truth serum worked every time, but in order for it to be effective, the serum had to be *in* her vein. He grunted in frustration, watched the car drive away with Camille inside, and headed to the exit. Next time. There was always a next time.

❖❖❖

Tope, Sawyer, and Camille sat down together in a small conference room at the station. Sawyer's office was too small to seat the three of them comfortably, so they opted for the conference room.

"I really don't know where to start," Camille began.

Sawyer took the lead and began the interview. "Let's start with your father. He gave you documents to keep safe, correct?"

Camille sighed. "Yes and no. Nine months ago, just before he died, my father entrusted me with two separate documents, both in some kind of code. One was two pages, the other was a single page. I have no idea what they said."

"Were you aware of his stolen identity?"

"I kind of remember my father telling me when I was very young that my name would be Camille Cofford. I knew that name was different from the name I'd always had, but I was so little."

"And what was your name prior to being called Camille Cofford?"

Camille twisted in her chair and struggled to answer the question. The name had been banned in her family; no one ever spoke of the old name. Not only was she surprised at how difficult it was to say, she was surprised she even remembered the name.

"Janae. My name was Janae Manning."

Tope did everything he could to maintain a calm face. He knew that name from his conversation with Patrick and Cayman prior to leaving D.C., but not only that. He knew it from his course of study when he entered the FBI. That was a big case, an old case.

Tope looked at Sawyer and his mind raced. *How am I going to handle this? I can't call D.C. and check in with Cayman or Patrick, or anyone for that matter.*

"Sawyer, can I have a word?"

"We'll be right back." Sawyer smiled and touched her arm. "Can we get you anything to drink? Are you hungry?"

"No, no I'm not. Thank you."

As soon as the two men were in the hall, Tope practically dragged Sawyer back to his office and shut the door.

"Does that name ring any bells to you?" His eyes were wide and he could feel himself sweating.

"No, not particularly," Sawyer shook his head, far more calmly than Tope felt at the moment. "Should it?"

Tope began to pace back and forth in front of Sawyer's desk. "That's probably because we were pretty much babies when that whole thing came down."

"And?"

"Sawyer, Camille's mother, was Miriam Manning. I would bet on it. She sold secrets to the Russians and was sentenced to death in the electric chair. After her death, the husband and daughter just disappeared. I have a file I'm supposed to be reviewing on the Manning case, but I haven't had the time to really look at it. If she is who I think she is, we're going to have a real problem. I was told about this before I left D.C. and told that one agent couldn't work it alone, that it was too dangerous."

"Well, then, you're not alone. You have me."

"Sawyer, I don't even know if I'm supposed to be telling you anything about this. I don't think *anyone* is supposed to know anything about this. I'm really not even sure how to proceed from here."

"Okay, then I say we proceed with caution. We'll keep this one under our belts for now, finish questioning Camille and take what we find to the captain."

"I just don't know if that's what we should do; but before we decide that, yes, let's finish with Camille. I have to think this through really well and review the file before we involve anyone else in this."

Sawyer smiled. "Come on, Tope. Don't you think you're being a little overdramatic? It sounds a little too James Bond for me."

Tope ran his hand through his hair and stopped mid-stride. "It *is* James Bond, Sawyer. It *is* James Bond."

The men returned to the conference room to find Camille pacing the floor.

They all sat back down at the table and she stared at both men before she spoke. "I don't understand. I told you my old name. What is the significance of that? Why all the sudden secrecy? My dad never told me a thing."

Tope took over the interview. "Camille, how did you lose your mother?"

"She died in childbirth. She died giving birth to *me*. I never knew her, and my father never kept pictures of her or of the two of them. I don't even know what she looked like. All my life it only was just the two of us. Mother was never a word we used at our house. Almost like she never existed, like I never really had one."

"And you're unaware why that was the case?"

Camille was becoming agitated with the line of questioning. "Of course I'm unaware. What are you keeping from me? What do you know that I don't know? My father told me nothing of my mother. She died in childbirth. That's all I know. Do you know more than that? For years I've wondered why I've lived this secret life. My father died with no explanation for it. If you know something, you tell me now or I'm out of here and I will melt into America and you'll never find me."

"Okay, Okay. I'll tell you as much as I can, but once I do, you'll be restricted in where you can go and who you can talk to. Obviously this Clyde Naples is trying to get his hands on you and that is the piece I don't have an answer for. You do. I'm certain of it. Whether you know it or not, you have the answer."

"Go on." Her words were clipped and hard.

"Your name is Janae Manning. Your father was Arthur Manning. Your mother…your mother was…Miriam Manning. Does that name mean anything to you?"

"No it does not. Why should it? I told you I never knew my mother. I told you she died in childbirth and my father wouldn't ever sp-"

"She didn't die in childbirth, Camille." Tope's voice was quiet, level, sure.

"What are you talking about? Of course she did! Are you calling my father a liar?" Camille's voice level was rising as she spoke and her body language screamed agitation.

"Camille, I know this is hard to hear. I know it is, but you have to calm down. You have to listen very closely to what I have to say. You have been keeping a secret for a very long time, haven't you? There is something you know that Mr. Naples needs to know. I don't know if it's in your head or written down somewhere, but you know something, and I'm fairly certain that 'something' is dangerous to you.

Camille's voice dropped to a whisper, her eyes wide with disbelief. "How could you know that? How could you know I'm carrying a secret? No one knows that, even Tug didn't know it."

Chapter Seventeen

"What did he tell you, Camille? What are you hiding?"

"I…I can't. I don't trust you; I can't trust you. I can't trust anyone."

"Camille, I'm going to tell you something that could cost me my life, because I want you to know that I trust you."

Sawyer stepped in. "Stop, Tope. Stop right there. A word, please."

Tope's eyes never left Camille's. "I'll be right back."

Sawyer stepped out of the conference room and, fearing Camille would flee out of a panicked fear, locked the door from the outside, slipping the key into his pocket. This time, it was Sawyer dragging Tope back to his office. Nearly slamming the door, Sawyer turned on Tope in a quiet rage.

"Are you kidding me?" The whispered words hissed from his mouth. "You're about to tell her who you are and why you're here, aren't you? You can't give her that, Tope, you don't even know if she's one of the good guys or bad guys. You don't even know if you can *TRUST* her, Tope. What are you thinking?"

"You and I both know we'll never get a step closer to solving this thing without the piece she's keeping secret. Even the NSA isn't cracking this code, and if it's got that big an encryption on it, it's important. We need to know what she knows. If one of us dies, it's better than losing a whole country, isn't it?"

The silence in the room was thick. Sawyer's eyes bored into Tope's. Neither man flinched.

"I lost your uncle who was like a brother to me, Tope, and I won't let the same thing happen to you. I won't."

Tope dropped his head and turned it to the side, staring at the desk. He raised his head and turned back to Sawyer before speaking. "I have a choice in this, Sawyer. I have the right to tell her what I need to tell her. My gut tells me this is going to be fine. My brain says run. I've always trusted my gut over my brain. Now let's finish this."

Tope strode to the door and opened it, stepping out into the bullpen.

"Tope, Tope stop!" Sawyer hurried after, but there was no stopping him. Tope was a man on a mission now, and he had a job to do.

With an angry frown, Sawyer slipped the key into the lock on the interrogation room door and pushed it open. Camille was still sitting at the table, her back stiff, her eyes focused straight ahead. She didn't move when they entered.

Tope came around the table and sat down in front of Camille. Her eyes eventually came to rest on his face.

"Camille, I work for the FBI out of Washington D.C. I came here because I was involved in an operation and my cover was blown. The people we were investigating want me dead for betraying them. If they find out where I am, they will send people to kill me. If you want me dead, all you have to do is tell them and I'm a dead man. I'm trusting you with my life. Will you trust me with yours?"

Camille's eyes widened. "You're FBI?" She seemed stunned by the information.

"Yes I am."

Camille dropped her face into her hands and sobbed. Tope wondered if he'd done the right thing in telling her about him.

He stood, picked up his chair, and carried it around the table. He placed it next to Camille, facing the side of her chair. Leaning into her, he spoke softly.

"Camille, the information you have could save the country. It has to be important for you to put such thought into sharing it. Your father did an excellent job of impressing upon you how important it is."

Camille raised her head. Her eyes were red, her makeup running down her face. She was the most beautiful woman he'd ever seen.

"My father told me that one day I would find someone I could trust with this information. I thought that person was Tug, I'm sure it was Tug. Now he's dead and…and I feel like he knew more about what I was hiding then he let on. I don't know how or why, but he knew."

"What do you mean?"

"I was going through Tug's files today and I found one that had a funny label. It felt empty and I was going to toss it into the garbage, but I opened it and the file contained the same message my father gave me. It was the exact same handwriting. But I *burned* that note, just like my father said to do. This one must be some kind of photocopy, but I can't figure out how Tug had it in his possession, or *why* he would have it. My father made me believe it was the only copy in the world."

Tope reached around her shoulders and gave her a squeeze. "I have to tell you the rest of the story of your family, Camille. You mother was put to death as a traitor. She died in the electric chair. Your original family name, Manning, is known and studied at government training facilities."

Camille jumped from her chair and backed away from both of the men. "You're lying. You want to know what I know, so you're lying to me to get what you need. My mother died in childbirth. She died giving life! You're a liar! You're both liars!"

She turned and ran for the door, but Sawyer got to the door first. "I can't let you leave now, Camille. We are not lying. We can show you the records online."

Tope stood and spoke slowly, trying to calm Camille. "I'd be willing to bet that your mother died protecting this country, not betraying it. There was a reason she and your father couldn't let this information out and we may never know what that was. But maybe you can change her status on her records. Maybe, if you can tell us what you know, she will no longer be known as a traitor. I can't promise that, because I don't know what the information is that you have. However, your father thought it important enough to protect all these years."

"I have to think. I want to go back to the hotel so I can think."

"It's not safe for you to go back there, Camille," Tope took another step toward her but she shrank into the wall, bringing her hands to her chest as if to make herself melt into it. He continued, "I'm not going to hurt you, you know that. We're trying to help you. You have to trust us, Camille. You have to trust *someone.*"

Camille stood pressing her side against the wall as if she were trying to escape into it. Tope couldn't figure out why she would be so afraid. What could be so big that she would be this frightened to tell anyone? Then a thought struck him. *Is she afraid of the information she has, or afraid for the safety of anyone she gives it to?*

"Camille, come back and sit down," Sawyer said, motioning to the table. "Let's figure this out. It's time for you to have a life, to stop carrying this burden, this secret you've been keeping. Come. Sit down. Please."

The woman sighed, exhaustion manifesting itself as her body relaxed. Tope put his arm around her shoulders and helped her back to the table. Sawyer returned to the other side of the table and Tope stayed seated beside her. Once Camille started talking, the words poured from her mouth.

"I don't even know what it means, really. It's just a jumble of letters and numbers but Daddy said it was important…very important. He also said it could 'clear' him and my mother and protect me. I didn't know what he meant. I'd really never even thought about that, but with what you've said, it makes perfect sense now." She sighed and stared at her hands. "I was living in shame, in hiding, and though I felt I was, I never actually knew I was. My father never said we should be ashamed, but I sensed shame from him. I'd always memorized exactly what I'd say if anyone ever suspected or found out. And when Tug was killed, there was no doubt in my mind that it was because of the two documents I'd given him. Imagine my shock when I found the note I'd *burned,* hidden in one of his files! He had to have said something to someone about it, about the documents, but I can't imagine he did. He was a good man who loved his country. He would die before he'd tell anyone what he knew."

Her eyes filled with tears as she gazed at Tope. "I guess that's exactly what happened. I don't understand it."

This information required a whole new line of questioning and Tope began back at the beginning of the interview.

"How long had you known Tug, Camille?"

Camille's shoulders slumped again. "I'd known him for six months, I met him three months after my father died. When Tug died I'd only worked for him for three days. I was afraid to tell you that because I thought you'd think I killed him."

"We would have asked a few more questions before we came to that conclusion, Camille. How did the two of you meet?"

"I was sitting on a park bench and Tug sat down and started up a conversation with me, and then everywhere I went, there he was. Always friendly, always ready to visit. I just figured it's because the town was small, but now I wonder."

"Did you ever feel like he was stalking you?"

"No, never. It wasn't like that. He was just a really nice guy, and he always seemed as surprised to see me as I was to see him."

"Did the two of you ever…connect? Were you dating him?"

"No, not at all. He was so much older than me, and more like a father figure, though he was dating a woman my age. I never considered him anything but a close friend and father figure."

"How did the topic of the documents come up?"

Camille began to blush. Clearly embarrassed, she began. "It seems so stupid now, like I was some naïve school girl or something. But I trusted him. I had no reason to doubt his motives."

Looking from Sawyer to Tope, she continued. "One day he told me he had this incredible safe he'd just built and how secure it was. He kind of laughed and told me if I had anything of value he'd be happy to store it for me. Just like that, and I didn't even suspect him at all. He let me put them in the safe and he locked it up and that was that. It felt really good to not have them in my possession. I know at some point he moved the decryption page to the bank vault. He told me he'd done this to protect the documents, because both documents shouldn't ever be in the same place. I trusted him and never questioned him about that decision. I should have. He suspected something, I was sure of it, but he said nothing."

"You said Clyde Naples had started coming to your home, bothering you. When did that start?"

Camille thought for a moment. "It was probably a day or two before I met..." Her voice trailed off. She stared from Tope to Sawyer and back to Tope. "He knew. Tug knew about Clyde Naples. That's why he befriended me. He was-"

"Protecting you," smiled Tope, finishing her sentence. "And protecting his country."

"Do you think he approached Mr. Naples and told him to stop bothering me? Do you think that's what got him killed?"

Tope sat back in his chair, thinking, and Sawyer started back into the conversation.

"You know, Camille," he began, "Tug was a man of action, and he'd fought in a tough war. I doubt there was much he was afraid of. I think Tug somehow knew what those documents meant. That is going to take some serious investigating, but we'll figure it out. For now, our job is to keep you safe."

"Camille, we need to know what was on that note you memorized." Tope brought the conversation abruptly back to the beginning. "You need to tell us so we can get it to the people who can figure this whole thing out."

Far more comfortable now than she had been, Camille reached into her shirt and pulled the note from her bra. She smiled innocently. "It was the only place I felt it would be perfectly safe."

She handed the note to Sawyer and Tope rose, walking around the table to peer over Sawyer's shoulder.

Camille had been correct, as she would be, having memorized it years before. It was a series of not just numbers and letters but symbols. One line, underlined and handwritten. Some of the symbols were single underlined, others double, and then the whole line was underlined. It meant nothing to either man, nor did it mean anything to Camille. Still, the fact that it was out of her hands gave her a sense of euphoria that was hard to miss.

"You look like someone who's been unjustly imprisoned and just released." Tope smiled at her, pleased for her freedom.

"That's exactly how I feel," she said, beaming. "I had no idea it would feel this good to let go of *all* of it. No more secrets. No more pretending. It's all over and done."

Sawyer had been staring at the line on the paper. "Now *our* work begins. But first, we have to find a place for you. You are going underground, Miss Cofford."

Chapter Eighteen

The man they called Clyde Naples stood and stretched. It was morning and he'd slept really quite well, safe in his underground hideout which was, literally underground. The old house was unassuming and weather beaten and looked abandoned except for the oversized lock on the front door. The basement had been transformed early on into a high tech spy nest, and had all the computer equipment and gadgets one would need to conduct an operation that needed to be 'discreet.'

If his employers knew how the last few days had gone down, they'd probably send someone to kill him and take over the operation. His name was out there now, but it wasn't his real name, fortunately. There were far too many people who knew he was in town and looking for the documents belonging to one Camille Cofford. He'd found her fast enough, and if he was any good at what he did, he was certain her real name, her real *last* name was Manning, daughter of

Arthur and Miriam Manning. Those two, Arthur and Miriam, were the key to everything.

There was no way this one time spy couple left this earth without telling their daughter the story of who they were and what they had. With the death of Arthur, she became the one with the key, whether she knew it or not. However, he'd bet good money she knew, at least some of it, if not all of it.

Naples strode to the computer room and settled in at the workstation. He composed an email, short and to the point, as instructed, then coded the email and pressed send. It wasn't much, but it was an update. By this evening, he'd have the documents in his hand and be out of this slice of Mayberry and headed home. He hadn't seen his family in weeks and he missed them.

He stood and strode into the kitchen area and poured himself a cup of his favorite coffee, Panama Elida Natural Gold Label. It was only minutes before the whole space filled with the wonderful aroma of fresh brewed, premium, coffee. He couldn't afford this luxury when he was home, mostly because his wife would ask how he could afford such extravagance. Too many questions were not good on the home front. But when he was on an operation, his employer covered all his expenses and he ate and drank in total opulence, enjoying every minute of it. He loved his family, but the money he made on these jobs was his own.

Settling down in his favorite easy chair, Naples rested his head on the seat back and closed his eyes. Today he would shut this operation down and be done with it. He'd messed with it enough, tried to be polite but no one was helping. So, now he'd get serious.

Word on the street was that he was the one who killed the Marine. Whatever. *I don't know who killed the guy, but it wasn't me. He shouldn't have taken a shine to the Manning kid. That had to be what got him killed. Had to be. Probably a jealous boyfriend or something.*

He opened his eyes and sipped his coffee, scanning his comfortable surroundings. This was a great little safehouse. Of all he'd used, this one was his favorite. He thought it might be nice to keep this one around and use it for a little get away someday. *Like that would ever happen.*

He took a last slurp of coffee, then drained the cup. He stood, strolled lazily back into the kitchen and placed the cup in the sink. There were plenty of dirty coffee cups in the sink, which he promised himself he would stick in the dishwasher before he left. He always left his safehouse the way he found it.

Sitting down at the computer once more, Naples took a small flash drive from a drawer in the computer desk. He inserted it into the USB port on the side of the monitor and entered a password into the program on the screen. When the needed information popped up, he reviewed it then saved it to the flash drive. Once finished he removed the flash drive, placed it in a small box and placed the box in a hidden pocket of his coat.

After shaving, showering and dressing, he went to the door leading upstairs. He glanced around the area one more time.

"See you tonight," he said, shaking his head as he headed up the stairs. *I'm way too attached to this place.*

Once at the top of the stairs, the ambiance was gone. The house was empty, dusty and dilapidated. It didn't look like it'd had decent care even when someone lived there. The smell was disgusting. He hurried to the front door, keyed in the code that unlocked the outside lock, and opened the door. He replaced the lock before heading to his car, which was safely stowed behind the nearly collapsed barn.

The car was not much to look at, but in a town like Blakely one had to keep a low profile. The fancy sports cars he usually drove were for the larger cities that required more finesse. This town had no finesse, and his car was rolling proof.

Approaching the car, he pressed the button to unlock the door and grabbed the handle to open it. Before he could lift the handle, a jolt of electricity traveled swiftly from his fingertips, up his arm and through his body. He cried out involuntarily as the current raced to his heart, stopping it nearly before the cry left his lips.

The man who called himself Clyde Naples lay in a crumpled pile beside his car. Burns on his fingers and up his arms filled the air with a putrid stink, but he didn't smell it.

Hidden in the barn, a giggle escaped joyful lips as nimble fingers dialed 911. Once the death was called in so the body could be found, this would be a job well done. For the time being, anyway. Still so much to be done yet. So very much to be done.

❖❖❖

The call came into the department just as Tope and Sawyer were returning from getting Camille tucked safely away in a hotel room adjoining Tope's. In a place as small as Blakely, there weren't many options. They had two officers posted outside her door 24 hours a day.

The unnamed caller said there was a body at an old farmhouse outside of Blakely. From the description of the place, it was the Tucker farm, abandoned for nearly thirty years.

When they arrived at the location there was no caller in sight. Disturbing to both investigators, they strode to the barn as instructed and found the car in the back. Sawyer reached for the door handle as Tope was studying the body.

"STOP!" Tope screamed at his friend. "Don't touch that car. Check out his fingers."

"He was electrocuted," mused Sawyer. "You think the car did this?"

"I've seen this before," replied Tope. "It's used a lot by the mob. They hook up the battery so the current runs through the body of the car. It kills pretty fast."

Tope squatted down to inspect the body. "Do you recognize this guy?"

"No, not really. Do you?" Sawyer covered his mouth and nose to mask the smell of the charred remains.

"This is the infamous Clyde Naples."

Sawyer stared at the face of the dead man. "Well, well. We finally meet. Maybe now we can figure out who he really is and who he's working for." Sawyer scanned the barn and farmhouse. "He was obviously about to go somewhere, eh?"

"Is that a lock on the front door?" Tope squinted in the sun toward the farmhouse. The CSI team was pulling up the drive. They parked by the barn and hurried to where Sawyer and Tope were standing.

Sawyer directed them to the body with a stern warning about the car. "We're going to check out the house. Looks like there's a lock on the door. This place hasn't been locked in decades."

Luke Golding, CSI lead nodded and put his team to work as the two detectives moved toward the house.

When Tope and Sawyer were within fifty feet of the house there was a huge explosion that rocked the ground, tossing pieces of the old farmhouse through the air like toys. The force of the blast threw the two detectives into their car parked in the open area a short distance from the house, and the CSI team ducked for cover. The barn somehow withstood the blast and no one was injured.

Tope heard little for the first few minutes after the blast. Every sound was muted, even the sound of falling debris. Sawyer looked at him and Tope knew he was experiencing the same thing. Neither man lost consciousness and the CSI team ran to help them.

"Can you hear me?" called Luke. "How many fingers am I holding up?"

"You're a little muted," replied Sawyer, "but we'll be fine. And eleven. You're holding up eleven fingers."

Luke looked concerned and Tope started laughing. "He's kidding, Luke. You should know Sawyer by now."

"That's not funny, Kingsley." Luke stood and returned to his team.

Tope was the first one on his feet. His head was spinning slightly but he could hear sounds gradually returning. He reached down to help Sawyer up and saw blood draining slowly from his left ear.

"I'm taking you to the hospital."

"I'm fine, don't be ridiculous. I don't need an arsenal. What are you thinking?"

Tope spoke a little louder. "I said hospital, not arsenal. You need to see a doctor."

Sawyer stared at him like he was talking nonsense. "A proctor? What is a proctor? We need to figure out why that building blew."

Tope finally yelled so Sawyer could hear him better.

"Get in the car. We'll call the fire department and Captain on the way."

"On the way to where?"

"GET IN THE CAR!"

They passed the fire truck and police cruisers as they pulled from the driveway onto the highway. Captain Amerson answered his phone after one ring. Tope explained what had happened and the captain said he'd head to the crime scene and meet up with Tope at the hospital when he'd completed his assessment of the scene.

Sawyer's surprise was evident when they pulled into the hospital parking lot. They walked into the ER with Tope still yelling to try to explain to Sawyer why they were there. Sawyer's hearing was improving some, but he still couldn't make out what Tope was trying to tell him, so Tope grabbed Sawyer's hand and ran his little finger over the blood coming from his ear. He stuck the bloodied finger in front of Sawyer's face so he could see what Tope was talking about. Sawyer nodded, a look of comprehension spreading slowly across his face.

The ER nurses hurried Sawyer into the trauma room and Tope called Esley to let her know where they were.

"Is he okay? I'll come right now. Will you watch Jack for me? No, wait, you can't watch Jack, you'll have to go right back out."

"Esley-"

"I'll get someone to watch him and I'll be right there. Is he talking? Is he conscious? How long was he out?"

"Esley-"

"You said he was bleeding, is he losing a lot of blood? I need to get there. I need to hurry-"

"Esley! Stop! I can't get a word in."

"Oh, right, sorry."

"Sawyer is going to be fine. They're checking him out. We both had hearing issues when the blast first happened, but mine is back and his is coming back. You don't need to worry."

"Okay, but I'm still coming down."

"I'll let him know you're on your way."

Tope ended the call and went to the desk. "Would you let Sawyer Kingsley know his wife is on the way?"

"Yes sir," replied the receptionist and picked up the phone to call back to the trauma room.

Tope sat down in the empty ER waiting area, pulled out his note pad and began writing down the day's events while they were still fresh in his mind.

Within a very few minutes Captain Amerson entered the ER and went straight to Tope. "How is he?"

"I haven't heard, but he walked in here with me, so I think he's going to be fine. He may have a concussion, but he'll be fine."

Captain Amerson sighed. "That's good news. Now to figure out what is going on with this investigation. Someone just killed the killer."

Chapter Nineteen

Captain Amerson sat down in the seat beside Tope, heavy with discouragement.

"One step forward, two steps back."

"Excuse me?" Tope stared at the captain. He'd not known him for that long, but he didn't seem like the kind of person to give up or get discouraged. Not that he was giving up, but he definitely sounded discouraged.

Captain Amerson rose and approached the ER desk. "Excuse me, I'm Captain Amerson with the Blakely Police Department. Can you direct me to a private room where my detective and I can talk?"

"Certainly, sir, I'll come around to the double doors and get you."

Amerson motioned for Tope to follow him and the nurse opened the large doors leading into the trauma rooms. She stopped in front of one of the small rooms and motioned for them to enter.

"Thank you, this will work perfectly." He smiled at the nurse and she returned to the front desk.

Once they were seated, Captain Amerson began.

"I heard back from the NSA on that cypher. I'd sent them the most recent information you got from Camille. They told me the original document had been plans for some equipment used by the military. However, the information was so old and the equipment was obsolete, they weren't sure why there was any interest in the document at all. When they got the new line of code, they inputted it into their decryption program and found a document *inside* the original document. It was a letter."

"A letter? To whom? *From* whom?"

Captain Amerson raised his hands in a helpless gesture. "Apparently to anyone who would listen and the 'from' portion is blacked out. It laid out quite clearly that Miriam Manning, along with her husband Arthur, were innocent of any wrongdoing and proves without a doubt that Miriam had stolen the document from a Soviet spy to *return* it to the United States Government. The NSA is keeping the name of the Soviet operative under wraps, why I don't know. Seems like the whole thing is a done deal. They'll be issuing a statement within the week as to the change in status of the Manning family."

Tope was confused. "That's good news then, right? But if it's good news, why wouldn't Mrs. Manning tell someone when it happened? What was the point of not sharing it so her life could be spared?"

Captain Amerson shook his head; sadness and grief blanketed his face. "She was protecting other operatives who were still out there. My contact at the NSA wouldn't say any more, just that she died protecting other operatives. It's a tragedy, and yet, an amazing story of heroism. She could have had her life spared and instead, chose to die to protect others. The code that Camille was hiding made that very clear."

Tope thought for a minute. "None of that makes sense. I mean, why did Arthur tell Camille that she would know when to share this information? Why didn't he just share it before he died so they could come out of hiding and clear the family name?"

Captain Amerson sat back in his chair and laced his fingers across the top of his head, resting his hands there. "I'm not sure Arthur knew what was in the second document. Without the proper computer program, I don't know that he *could* know, unless she told him. I think, if she was fearful of the government, of all the corruption she saw in her own organization, that she thought the less her family knew, the safer they would be. Still, she did entrust the main documents to his care, and somehow impressed upon him the need to keep the second document, the line of code, secret at all costs. The NSA is being extremely tightlipped about that whole part, but I'd be willing to bet there were still operatives out there that needed protection, and Mrs. Manning knew who they were. Maybe she also knew they would be retired or deceased in a few years time, and there would be no need for protection. I don't know if any of that's true, but it's a guess."

Both men sat silently for a minute before Captain Amerson spoke again. "You remember those two files you found in Tug's office? The ones with handwritten code in them?"

"Yeah, I do."

"Apparently Tug was trying to use the line of code he had in his possession to decode the document. However, it took a computer to do that. It is thought he feared for the country and was desperate to make sure the country and its operatives were safe. How he got that copy of the last line of code, they aren't saying. I'm guessing he was one of those operatives whose life was saved by Mrs. Manning. I'll bet he sought out Camille because Mrs. Manning told him who she was and the possible danger she would be in. When Naples hit town, Tug knew he had to protect her because he knew Naples. How, I don't know, but I'd be willing to lay money on that."

"Okay, but why would Naples go to such elaborate measures to get that line of code if it was going to erase any suspicion from the Mannings?"

"Because of the other operatives named in the embedded document found with that second line of code. If they could get that list, find out who and where they were, there was a chance they could sell that list of names to the highest bidder, that the information obtained from those operatives could still be useful. Nobody's saying at the NSA, but, again, that's my guess."

"And the two steps back?"

Amerson shook his head. "Who killed the killer? We have to find the person or persons responsible not only for Tug's death, but the Naples murder as well. I just don't get it, though.

The document is in the hands of the NSA; the last string of code is also there. Surely the killer has to know the jig is up, right? Are they really still after Camille? Why would they be? And who blew up the vault? We still don't know what happened to that cypher, even though it's useless now with the original document decrypted. Someone believed it to have value, and believed it strongly enough to risk breaking into that vault."

The doors to the trauma rooms opened and Sawyer was wheeled into the waiting area, free to leave. In a wheelchair. And he was *not* happy about it.

"This is ridiculous. I can *walk* to the car, you know. I walked *in* here." He complained all the way across the floor as the wheelchair rolled toward them.

"Rules are rules. I will see you to your car." The nurse was smiling. It sounded like she heard this complaint a lot.

"How's that chair working for you?" Tope smiled broadly. "Payback. I'm feelin' the love right now."

Sawyer scowled and mumbled, "Thanks, a lot."

"Can he work?" asked Amerson.

The nurse handed instructions to the closest person, who was Tope, and Sawyer tried to grab them away.

"Ah- ah- ah. I have a feeling you wouldn't be telling us the whole truth if we didn't have this in our hands."

Just as Tope began studying the instructions, Esley came jogging through the door. She saw Sawyer and hurried to him.

"Are you okay? Tope said you were going to be fine." Her eyes searched the nurse's face, and then Tope's and the captain's.

"He's going to be fine. He just needs some rest." The nurse smiled at Esley.

"Good luck with that," chuckled the Captain.

"Wow," said Tope, having scanned the paperwork. "Not so much as a concussion! His eardrum was torn a little, or something, but he's going to be fine."

Sawyer started to stand and the nurse gently pushed his shoulder so he remained in the wheelchair.

"Your car?" The nurse looked expectantly at the group before her.

Esley's face was somber, the fright still apparent on her face. "He's coming home with me," she said, staring pointedly at first Sawyer and then the captain. "He's not working anymore today." This was a statement of fact and everyone in the group knew better than to argue the point with her.

Captain Amerson nodded his approval and Sawyer was wheeled from the ER complaining the whole way. "Oh come on, Captain! I can walk and I can work. We have a lot to do. Captain!"

The doors closed behind him as they wheeled him out to the family car. Captain Amerson chuckled. "It'll do him good to rest. He'd work himself to gray hair if I let him. Let's go get some dinner, it's been a long day."

"You buyin'?"

"I see Sawyer has trained you well," he chuckled. "Yes, I'll buy. It's the least I can do after you saved the man's hearing. Although, he's not going to forgive either of us for allowing his wife to take him home. He considers us both traitors, now, for sure."

Captain Amerson drove to the diner and Tope followed him in his car. Once they were seated, Tope asked a question that had bothered him since he'd left the hospital.

"Captain, I was thinking; *if* Mrs. Manning knew Tug, *if* he was on that list of names…could she have given him that note with the last line of code?"

"I suppose it's possible, but to what end? That is the one question that's been keeping me up. How and why did Tug have that code? I don't think the cypher was ever the reason for all this in the first place. I think that second line of code, the one Camille memorized, was the actual target. I wonder if the person who blew up the vault thought that last line of code was in Tug's safe deposit box."

The waitress took their order and both men sat deep in thought once she left. Captain Amerson finally broke the silence.

"Funny how you get to the end, or sort of to the end, of an investigation like this and it leaves a nasty taste in your mouth. I've never had that happen before. Of course, it's not over yet, but why isn't it?"

"So, let's think this through, Captain," Tope began. "The documents are decrypted, they're at the NSA, the Manning name is cleared, Camille's secret is out, Naples, or whatever his name is, is dead. What we need to do is examine that crime scene once the fire is out and cooled. What made that house explode? Who killed Naples? Who killed Tug? *IS* Camille still in danger? Those are the major things that are left now, am I right?"

"Sounds right to me."

The waitress returned with their meals and after placing them on the table, left them to eat. Steak was the order of the day this time, and the two men dug in.

"Do you think we'll uncover anything at the Naples crime scene?" Tope stuck a chunk of steak in his mouth and chewed thoughtfully.

"I think that's the next thing you and Sawyer are going to examine. If we're going to get any answers to this whole mess, it's going to have to start at that old house."

"Will he be ready to go out tomorrow, once the fire has cooled and we can sift through it?"

The captain scoffed. "He's ready *today*. If we try to keep him down longer than that, he'll be eating his family alive. I'm sure Esley is already trying not to kill him. He's not a nice patient."

They finished their meal and Captain Amerson paid the tab, then headed for home. Tope was anxious to check on Camille and tell her what was found. He decided to talk with Camille first and then go visit Sawyer.

Before he left, Captain Amerson turned back to Tope on the sidewalk outside the diner. He placed his hand on Tope's shoulder. "I know you want to tell Camille this extraordinary news, but you have to understand something. This is going to be a double-edged sword for her. Take it slow."

"Oh, I don't think so, Captain. She is going to be so relieved. I'm sure of it."

"Tread carefully. That's all I'm saying. Take it slow and tread very carefully."

Chapter Twenty

In spite of the captain's warning, Tope could hardly contain his joy for Camille. She'd lived a life of secrets and carried a heavy burden with these documents entrusted to her care. She was hiding something and felt the weight of that responsibility, never knowing the sacrifice her mother had made for those pieces of paper. When Sawyer and Tope told her of her mother's death, she took it very hard. What an honor to now tell her that her mother was a hero and that heroism would soon be made public. Camille would finally know the full truth about her family and about Tug.

Arriving at his room he greeted the two officers tasked with keeping Camille safe. They reported there had been no activity and the room remained quiet all day. Tope unlocked his door and went inside. He knocked on the adjoining door.

Camille came to the door, her eyes red and swollen from tears.

"Camille! What's wrong?"

"I…I can't do this anymore, Tope. I've decided to move. I'll go somewhere where no one knows me and start over. I don't even have a job here anymore. I can sell my home and-"

"Camille, stop. Stop. You need to hear what I have to say."

"Why? It's just more bad news, and it feels like it keeps getting worse."

"Please, sit down." Tope motioned toward the easy chair and Camille saw the look on his face for the first time.

"Wha- what's happened?" Camille was staring at him now.

"I spoke with Captain Amerson tonight, and he had some news about your family, some really wonderful news!"

"What news?" Her eyes held hope for the first time since he'd known her.

"Your mother was as much a hero as Tug was, Camille. She died so she could save agents still in the field. The reason she had the documents your father gave you is because she'd stolen them back from those who'd taken them in the first place. People who only wanted to sell them to the highest bidder. But she couldn't let anyone know that she'd actually stolen them back, not even her own people. With the documents you had, the specialists at the NSA were able to finally decrypt the original document that was, at first decryption, only decommissioned and obsolete military equipment."

Camille was trying to be patient, but the information wasn't making sense to her and she was losing patience. "What was the big deal about old equipment? Who would kill for that kind of information?"

"That's what I'm about to tell you. They couldn't understand why anyone would want that old information. But when they input the single line of code you gave us, it revealed a document *inside* the original document. That second document was a letter absolving your mother of any wrongdoing, and it also contained a list of operatives who'd aided in the return of the original document, the document your father gave you to keep safe. Your mother was so concerned for the safety of those men and women on that list, she couldn't allow it to be discovered, not even by her own people. She was fully aware of the number of operatives selling secrets, at least the ones who'd been caught. She had to wonder how many *hadn't* been discovered. So she hid it away and died in shame to save the lives of those operatives, who are all either retired or deceased now."

"Wait. Wait," Camille stood and started pacing the room. "You're telling me, my mother was sent to the electric chair to save these other operatives? You're telling me she'd rather have died than told even her own government about the list of names?"

Tope didn't like where this was going. He could see her anger rising and Captain Amerson's words were beginning to ring in his ears. "Camille, come back and sit down. You have to understand the history of the time."

Camille returned to her seat, her blue eyes now red, swollen and *angry*.

"Your mother was an operative at a time in our history when there were people selling government secrets to make money. They were literally selling their country out. Your mother couldn't take a chance on these secrets getting out and causing more deaths, just so someone could line their pockets. She was a patriot, Camille. Pure and simple."

"Tug. Did Tug know about this?"

"We don't know for sure, the NSA is keeping the details quiet as yet, but both Captain Amerson and I suspect Tug was one of the names on that list. It would make sense that his only way to repay Miriam Manning for her sacrifice was to make sure her daughter lived on. I've never been a parent, Camille, but I would imagine if I had a child who was in danger, that would be my one wish, to keep my child safe."

Tope watched as the wheels spun inside Camille's head. The hope he'd seen initially was gone, replaced with a sadness that looked deep and heavy. He leaned forward as she began to speak, taking her hands in his.

"I don't even remember my mother. I was a baby when she died. We couldn't even have pictures of her in our house! Now I understand that my father had to hide her away, so we could hide away. We couldn't even use our own family name. What kind of a country does that to a family? What kind of people would allow something like this to happen? Why? I was only a child. I needed my mother; my father needed his wife. We were a *family.* Or at least we could have been a family."

Tope hated seeing her like this. "It wasn't the 'people' who allowed this to happen, Camille. It was your mother, and she did it to protect military secrets of the time and operatives who were in danger of discovery. You did exactly what she would have wanted you to do. You kept the information and you gave it to the right person."

Camille pulled her hands away from Tope's and sat back in her seat, exhaustion evident. "I need some time to think. I need to be alone, Tope. I hope you don't mind."

"I understand. I'm going to see how Sawyer is doing. We were involved in a bit of trouble today and he was sent home to rest. You're welcome to ride along if you like." He didn't see the need to tell her the whole story at this time. She had enough to digest.

"No, you go ahead. I think I'm going to lie down for a while."

Tope rose and Camille stayed in her chair, gazing out the window. He left her sitting there and closed the adjoining door behind him. It was difficult not to stay with her, but he knew she needed some time, and she certainly deserved it.

Tope arrived at Sawyer's home to find a very irritable Sawyer, and a disgusted Esley. Their heated discussions prior to his arrival were evident, and plainly manifested on each of their faces. Jack was the only one who wasn't unhappy. He giggled and ran to Tope who picked him up and swung him through the air.

Esley stood next to Tope in the front entry of their home. Her arms were folded across her chest and she looked like she wanted to use Sawyer for a kicking bag.

"Good luck talking to him. He's in rare form tonight." She pulled Jack from Tope's arms and headed to his room amidst screams and cries.

Jack gradually calmed with promises of a fun bath and toys in the water. His cries faded as water started running in the bathtub.

"Hey Tope! What have you heard?" Sawyer acted like he'd been in the walls of his home for weeks instead of the few hours it'd been. Tope filled him in on what the captain had told him and how he'd rehearsed the whole thing to Camille.

"I'm sure she took that pretty hard."

"Yeah, I guess it surprised me. I was sure she'd be happy, even thrilled about it, but the more I tried to explain, the angrier she got. She said she needed some alone time, so I came to see how you were doing."

"Good plan. What's on the agenda for tomorrow?" Sawyer was like a wild horse ready to race the plains.

"Captain Amerson wants us to go through the debris of the farmhouse and see what we can find. It didn't look to me like there was much left, but you never know. What time do you want to meet out there?"

"Is five-thirty too early?"

"Yes."

"Fine, I'll meet you there at eight. Weenie." Sawyer grinned at his partner.

"Yeah, says the one who got to rest all day. I'm glad you're doing well. I'll see you out there at eight."

As Tope slid into the driver's seat of his car, his cell phone rang.

"Daniels."

As he listened to the caller he threw the car door open and jumped from the car. He raced up the walk to Sawyer's front door and threw it open.

"Camille's gone. She waited until one of the officers guarding her door left to use the bathroom, knocked the other one out and took off. We don't even know if she's safe out there yet! Whoever killed Naples and Tug could still be looking for her."

Chapter Twenty-One

With Camille's sudden exit, Captain Amerson told Sawyer and Tope they were not to spend any extra effort searching for her. Unless she was proved to be involved in the murders somehow, they couldn't force her to stay tucked away from danger. If she wanted to be out there, there was nothing they could do to stop her.

Tope couldn't go against a direct order, even though technically he was just an advisor in this case and not an employee of the police department. Camille remained missing. It took every ounce of strength to keep himself on task and not run off on his own. However, what he did in his free time was his own business, at least that was his line of reasoning.

It had been nearly two full days since the explosion at the farm. Tope and Sawyer were in Sawyer's office right at eight the next morning as agreed, staring at the evidence board. According to the fire department, the burn site would finally be cool enough to investigate this afternoon. There was nothing to do but wait, and brainstorm. Tope posed the first question.

"We believe it was Naples that killed Tug Carlson, right?"

"Yes, why? What are you getting at? And you seem awfully at ease, considering Camille is out there somewhere, unprotected."

Tope stood and moved the word "Naples" under the name Tug Carlson.

"Well..." Tope stared at the board before beginning, "she's an adult, she can take care of herself. Now, we know Naples was after the documents that Tug had, correct?"

"Yes." Sawyer studied his partner. Tope wasn't being entirely honest, and though Sawyer had only met him just over a month earlier, he was fairly certain there was more to this story.

Tope continued staring at the board and suddenly spun around to face Sawyer who was sitting at his desk. "We need to exhume Arthur Manning."

"*What?*" Sawyer sputtered. "Where did that come from?"

Tope went slowly to his chair across from Sawyer, clearly still thinking the process through. He sat down and his eyes studied the evidence board.

"With everything we've seen in this case, Tug's murder, the explosion at the bank, the sniper's nest, Camille's story, Tug's attempt to decipher the code, Naples' murder, and now Camille's disappearance...with all this insanity, what makes you think Arthur Manning died of natural causes? People were trying to get to the information Manning had in his possession.

Someone somehow found out he had those documents and wanted them desperately enough to kill for them. When Arthur died, at least one person showed up on Camille's doorstep almost immediately, demanding to see those documents. Who knows if there were others waiting in the wings to snatch them up as soon as they found the opportunity."

"Yeah, so where are you going with this?"

"The chances that Mr. Manning died of natural causes are incredibly slim, in my experience, and if he didn't die of a heart attack, then who killed him?"

Sawyer had been rolling a pencil back and forth over his knuckles as he listened to his partner. He tossed the pencil onto his desk in frustration. "Great, just what we need. Another murder. Why would it matter who killed Manning at this stage of the game? With Naples gone, we don't even know *who* we're after now. For all we know, Naples killed Manning as well as Tug."

"Yes, and if someone was trying to get those documents, they would want Manning out of the way. They just hadn't planned on his daughter fighting back like she has. *AND* if we exhume the body, we can see if there is poison in the tissue and, possibly, find out where it came from, which might lead us to Manning's killer." Obviously pleased with his plan, Tope smiled confidently at Sawyer.

Sawyer sat back in his chair and a satisfied smile slowly creased his face. "Oh, *I* get it. If we exhume Camille's father, she's going to come out of her hiding place with boxing gloves on. You just want to find Camille."

"Not really. I already know where Camille is."

"Oh, right, and my name's Cinderella and my shoes are glass."

"I'm serious. I'm betting she's holed up in some seedy little hotel by night, but by day she's at her father's grave. She was really close to him, and she even told me she sometimes thought she could hear him whisper to her. She's at his grave, I'd bet my paycheck on it."

"Then why, Mr. Romeo, haven't you been out there?"

"Well, duh, Mr. Married Man. She obviously needs some space. With Naples out of the way, she's more than likely out of the line of fire. I'm totally in touch with my feelings, an incredibly enlightened man, and I know these things."

"You've talked with her."

"Yeah, pretty much."

"Why didn't you tell me?" Sawyer was out of his chair and standing now, angry. "Are we partners or not?"

"I did talk to her, but she didn't talk back," sputtered Tope. "There was nothing to tell. She's running scared, Sawyer, and she doesn't know what to do or where to turn. She's alone in the world, and she feels there is no one she can trust. She needs to come in on her own when she has her head unscrambled a little bit."

Sawyer was no longer looking at Tope. He was staring at his office door.

"She's standing behind me, isn't she." Topes words were not a question, but a statement.

"Yes she is."

Tope stood and turned around. He offered his most charming grin and started to speak, but was immediately interrupted.

"Don't bother," said Camille. "You're right on all counts."

Tope cast a quick "told ya" glance to Sawyer. "I'm sorry this has become so overwhelming, Camille," said Tope. He nodded toward Sawyer, including him in his conversation as he continued. "We both are. We didn't mean to scare you off, but we just don't know who's out there and what their intentions were. We- I just wanted to keep you safe."

"I know, I know," she said, coming around Tope's chair and collapsing into it. "It's just so much chaos. I want my life back. I want to find another job and do my job every day, go home at night, pop some corn and watch TV. I…I just want my life back."

Sawyer pulled his chair around his desk and sat down next to Camille. "You've been given some pretty heavy things to deal with in the past few days. We're aware of how difficult this has been for you. What we need to ask you is, are you able to hang in there with us for a few more days while we trap a killer?"

"I haven't decided if I'm staying in Blakely or not," she said softly. "I might sell my house and move away, far away. Maybe even out of the country."

Sawyer stood and moved his chair back to the other side of the desk.

"I won't try to stop you, Camille. I'm only asking for a few more days before you make your decision. If we can get to the bottom of this investigation, find the perp and solve this whole sordid mess, you wouldn't have to move if you didn't want to. Are you with us?"

Camille stood and turned to Tope. "What do you think? Do you still think I'm involved somehow, hiding things from you? Can you trust me to stay and not meddle?"

Tope took her hands in his. "You know what I think, Camille. You know I want you to stay, but I would never ask that of you, unless it was something *you* wanted to do."

Camille smiled at him. She turned to Sawyer, her hands slipping out of Tope's grasp. "I'll stay and help anyway that I can, but if either of you so much as *thinks* about accusing me of being part of this, of telling any more half-truths, I'll be gone so fast you won't have time to blink. I told you everything I know, and I'm done with secrets. I love this country. I worked for a man who loved this country. Even for the short time I knew him, he showed me what it meant to love America. Remember that, because I know I sure will."

"Got it," said both men in unison. Sawyer thought this a good time to talk about the exhumation. He explained why they felt it was necessary and what would be accomplished. Camille's response was unexpected.

"I have no problem with that. If it further vindicates my family, do what you need to do. Just remember what I said before. I meant it. And I'm moving back into my house today. Right now. I've already cleared out the hotel room. If you need me, I'll be at my house, as I am currently unemployed."

Camille turned and strode confidently from the room.

"I guess she told *you*," chuckled Sawyer.

"Oh, right, like you didn't deserve any of that!"

Sawyer's phone rang with the news they'd been waiting for. The fire department had cleared the burn site at the old farm for the detective's investigation.

Arriving at the site, there wasn't much left to investigate. The fire burned so hot, most everything was ash.

"Hey Sawyer," called the fire investigator, Benjamin Hanson. The man was incredibly good looking, knew that as a fact of his life, usually had a different date every night of the week, and the false confidence in his voice irritated Sawyer to no end. The department had taken to calling him Handsome Hanson, most often with a scoff. The man, knowing he was eye candy, totally spoiled the presentation. "Over here. You need to see this."

Sawyer and Tope both stepped gingerly out of the ashes and strode to the car. Presumably this was Naples' car, as he was found dead beside it. Waiting for the ashes to cool had taken a lot of valuable time from the investigation and only now had investigators gotten to the search of the car.

As Sawyer and Tope approached, Hanson smiled and tossed something metal at the car. A huge spark flew from the side of the vehicle. "Guess we found the murder weapon."

"Uh, yeah, Hanson," said Sawyer, rubbing his pointer finger over his lip. "We kind of figured that out with the electrical burns on the victim's body."

"I *suspect* that to be the case," gloated Hanson, ignoring Sawyer's comment. "I believe once we get under the hood, we'll find the car has been booby trapped. Ugly way to die, no?"

"So the killer didn't just blow up his hideout, he electrocuted his victim with his own car. That's just rude." Tope stared at the car. "And such a beautiful automobile as well." He held his chin in one hand, staring at the old, fairly rusted vehicle with adoring eyes, obviously doing his best not to break out in full laughter.

Sawyer stared at his partner like he wasn't sure he even knew who he was.

"You scare me sometimes, Mr. Daniels. You really scare me."

Sawyer turned back to Handsome Hanson. "Have you determined how to undo the trap?"

"Yeah, I think so. We've got some car guys on their way now. We should have this safely in the station garage before the end of the day."

Sawyer thanked him and returned with Tope to the now cold ashes.

Tope grinned as they approached the remains of the farmhouse. "He's awfully full of himself, isn't he? It's really quite amusing."

Sawyer scoffed and continued to the house. They donned gloves and carefully began moving what pieces they could find, hoping to find anything that would give them an idea of what happened. Tope pointed to the only part of the house still standing.

"Looks like the house had a storm cellar. Can't imagine there'd be much left down there. Let's have a look."

Hanson hurried to where they were making their way to a large debris covered object still standing in the center of the home. Sawyer saw Hanson and moaned. Oblivious to his reception, Hanson started right in.

"We found an accelerant over in this corner of the house, apparently on the inside of the home." He pointed to what remained of the door. "The door was blown out and away from the fire, thus preserving it and allowing us to find a remote lock securing it to the frame. The door had to have been reinforced, along with the frame, for it to stay intact through that strong of a blast."

"What was this guy hiding? Who would need that kind of security on a broken down old farm house?" Sawyer stared at the door, studying the still intact lock.

"We thought about that," cooed Hanson, "and we found this, once the burn cooled enough."

He led them to the pile of debris they were originally heading for. As they removed the pieces of plywood, wooden posts and sheetrock, all of it charred and soaked, they found beneath it a metal enclosure. The enclosure itself was discolored from the fire, but still standing. It looked like a storm cellar made to withstand a tornado strength wind. However, once the men got closer to it, it was clear they were looking at a far more than that, with metal that appeared to be over an inch thick. The door looked like it would have been inside a closet, or pantry, from what was left of the frame around the area where it stood.

"Has anyone been down there?" Sawyer looked at the fire investigator.

"Nope. I made sure everyone stayed out." Handsome Hanson was quite proud of himself. "Besides, it's got a security pad installed. It's going to take someone who knows how to decrypt a security code."

"Thanks," replied Sawyer. Clearly Hanson didn't need more than that if his head was ever to fit inside another building of any size.

Hanson strolled off like he owned the place and Sawyer watched him go, shaking his head. "That guy is bucking for a promotion to detective, and if that happens I'm moving out of the state."

Tope chuckled. "He's quite pleased with himself."

"Quite."

Sawyer turned his attention to the keypad. "I'm guessing if the code is attempted too often, it will shut down, or turn off, or blow up or something."

Tope leaned over the keypad as Sawyer took a step back. "Yeah, something like that. Let me have a look."

He reached for the lock with both hands and held down one key while punching in several others. They heard a loud click and Sawyer started to run.

"What are you doing?" Sawyer yelled while running and jumping over the remnants of the fire. "You don't know if that's going to blow up or open up! Get out of there! Now!"

Chapter Twenty-Two

Tope stood where he was. "Oh ye of little faith."

When there was no explosion, Sawyer stopped and turned back around. "What did you do?"

"I guess I forgot to tell you that I'm a lock expert. Did I forget that? Obviously I did; and did anyone ever tell you that you run like a girl?"

Sawyer started laughing. "My wife says that occasionally, but she pays for it, as will you. I just have to figure out where and when." He approached the door and inspected the lock. "How did you do that?"

"Oh, I'm afraid that's a secret amongst us FBI lock expert types. If I told you-"

"Yeah, yeah, yeah," interrupted Sawyer, "you'd have to kill me. That's an old one, you know. You 'FBI types' need to get yourselves some new material."

"Well, that wasn't what I was going to say, but it will do."

Tope pulled the door open and lights came up from the foot of the stairs. "I can't believe this survived that blast. It's got to have its own electric, plumbing, and air filtration system. There's no smoke damage down here at all."

They started slowly down the stairs, moving carefully should they find any damage to the stairwell, but the steps remained firmly in place.

Sawyer looked in awe at the extravagant surroundings. "Do you suppose this was an intact storm cellar, or better yet, bomb shelter and someone converted it?"

"I have no idea, but it looks like I've found my new apartment."

"In your dreams." Sawyer was still trying to take in what they'd found. "This place is evidence."

"I can live in evidence. I don't mind a bit." Tope was making his way to the computer room. "Check this out."

As Sawyer moved to where Tope stood, Tope turned on the computer system to boot it up. Nothing happened. The screen came on, but it was blank. There was no Internet connection. Someone was aware their operative was no longer in charge of the system.

"Why didn't they just blow the hideout along with the house? It makes no sense they would keep all the equipment operational." Sawyer strode to the copy machine, which was also a scanner and printer. "This stuff wasn't cheap. This is all new. He couldn't have been here that long."

Tope, now in full FBI mode, began wandering through the apartment muttering to himself as he inspected the layout.

"I wonder if whoever blew up the house didn't know about the basement. Or, if he did, maybe he thought it would all go up with the house. Obviously, Naples' employer knew he was dead, or this equipment would still be working. Which leads me to wonder, did the bomber know Naples' employer? If he did, he would've known his bomb wouldn't be strong enough to blow the basement along with the house. Are these computer lines still hooked up to the original server? That would be easy to figure out. They have to have severed all communications. They're too smart not to have done that."

"Okay, you lost me somewhere in there," Sawyer was following Tope, listening to him mutter and weighing what he said. "You think the bomber knew Naples and knew his employer?"

"If he did, surely he'd know the amount of C4 he used to blow this place wouldn't blow the hideout below." Tope continued muttering.

"C4? Who said anything about C4?"

"*AND* why would he use an explosive that would leave residue at the scene? Except, yeah, C4 is pretty easy to use and can be found almost anywhere. Was this an amateur? I think not. This guy knew what he was doing. Well, sort of anyway. I would have done it way better."

"Will you stop muttering and tell me what in the world you're talking about?"

Tope stopped, only now realizing he'd been speaking out loud. "Oh, sorry. An unfortunate result of working alone for so long. I'm just making mental notes verbally."

"Oh, right. Like that makes any more sense than what you've been going on about. Talk to me! Tell me what you're thinking so I can hear all of it, not just pieces." Sawyer was quickly losing his patience, mostly out of a need to know what his partner was finding.

Tope went slowly over what he had been thinking as he perused the residence. "This was a living space, along with a workspace, completely self-contained with all the amenities anyone could need if they had to stay out of sight for a while. The stockpile of food and water is impressive, along with the computer equipment and the living space in general, though that part is certainly lavish for your average hideout."

In all the information they could glean from the home itself, there wasn't a single item that told them who Clyde Naples really was. The house had clothes, food and equipment, but nothing tying anyone to any part of it.

Tope was muttering again and Sawyer stopped him. "Speak up. What are you saying?"

"Sorry. Old habits. I was just thinking, I wonder if the bomber wanted us to find this hideout."

"If he knew it was in the house, why didn't he find it himself?"

Tope thought for a minute. "I don't know, but the only thing that makes sense is that the bomber thought Naples had something he wanted. Possibly the documents Naples was sent to collect. Maybe this bomber isn't aware the documents aren't in Blakely anymore."

"But Naples never did have the documents in his possession." Sawyer was trying hard to keep up with Tope's line of thinking.

"Yeah, that's true, but either Naples' killer was led to believe Naples had the documents, or he assumed Naples had them. Either way, I'd be willing to bet he wanted *something* in Naples possession and was unaware of the living space below the farmhouse."

"Since we know Naples never had the documents," said Sawyer, standing with arms folded in the center of the room. "So, does that mean Camille is in more danger than we thought?" Sawyer's concern sent warning bells ringing in Tope's head.

"It's possible. It's more than possible. If this new killer thinks the documents are still in Blakely, he could come after Camille. We need to check on her before we head back to the station." Tope had that itch growing between his shoulder blades again. "We need to get to her house ASAP."

The men raced up the stairs from the basement and closed the door, quickly setting the lock. They rushed to the car and sped down the driveway toward Camille's place.

Sawyer's words rang in Tope's ear. *As much as you want to believe you don't care, it can't be turned on and off that easily.*

It seemed to Tope that his feelings for Camille were as much a mystery to him as this case was. One minute he thought for sure she was who and what she said she was. Then the next minute, he was sure she was lying. Now, given the ultimatum she'd handed down, he was certain he could trust her and he felt surprisingly relieved by that revelation.

As they raced to her home, Tope knew his feelings for her had never changed. They were only bouncing back and forth between the forbidden and the accepted. Whether he was allowed to love her or not, he loved her. Though unspoken, he'd tried to deny his feelings for long enough. He would tell her as soon as he could. If she didn't feel the same way, so be it. He loved her. He knew that much was true; and as far as he was concerned, they couldn't get to her home fast enough.

❖❖❖

Camille tugged at the roller bag luggage as she tried to get it up the two steps to her front door. She only had luggage because once she was placed in the hotel she was only allowed back in her home to get more clothes. This, of course, was done accompanied by two uniformed police officers. *Like a kindergartner crossing the street. And for WHAT? I'm so done with this whole thing. If you were here Dad, I'd probably give you a good tongue lashing for making me responsible for the keeping of those stupid documents and line of code I memorized. What's done is done. I just want a nice cup of tea and some time to unwind from it all.*

With a final pull up the last and taller of the two stairs, she approached the door of her home and slid the key into the lock. Even hearing the key click open made her smile. This was *her* home and she was going to enjoy it. Even though it was still a complete mess from her encounter with Mr. Naples. Camille scoffed and opened the door.

To her surprise the house was clean and put back together. Even the broken lamps and pottery had been replaced with nearly the same item as she'd had. There was a note on the end table and she set her luggage upright, leaning over the couch to pick up the note.

"Camille;

We left the house in a bit of a hurry, and the front door was left unlocked. I hope you don't mind. I took the liberty of hiring a cleaning service to come and put the house back in order. I stayed with them while they cleaned. I figured when you got home you'd not be in the mood to clean up an ugly reminder of the events from that evening. Enjoy!

Tope

A smile brushed her lips as she held the note to her breast. What was it about Tope Daniels that made her go all tingly inside? Maybe it was that in her wildest dreams she'd never thought she'd find such an amazing man. He could definitely make a woman's heart beat a whole lost faster.

Leaving the luggage in the entry, Camille went into the kitchen and pulled a cup and saucer from the cabinet. Grabbing her teakettle from the stove, she filled it with water, replaced it, and turned on the unit.

Somehow, Camille felt…different. She'd always been a little timid, maybe even shy. But this whole experience had been terrifying, and when it wasn't terrifying it was frustrating and irritating. She was sure if one more person attempted to touch her she would pinch off their head. Somehow, she'd gained more confidence, or was it anger? Maybe she was fed up. But whatever it was, she was done; done with the whole stupid thing.

She returned to the cabinet and pulled out her small box of chamomile tea. She loved the way the china sounded as she picked up the saucer with the cup. There was something soothing about that sound, the china clinking against itself when the cup and saucer was moved. A memory from childhood? Not that she could remember. She just liked the sound of it. Sometimes a sound was just a sound.

Pulling a tea bag from the box, she placed it in the cup and turned to set it on the table. Only then did she realize she wasn't alone.

"I'll take one of those," said a weasel-like voice. The man smiled, his fat cheeks somehow making room for the broad grin.

A portly looking man stepped from the shadows, but Camille was surprisingly not surprised. Instead, she was just angry and still feeling quite done with everything.

"Get out. Get out now before I pick you up and set you on the porch like a scraggly cat."

The look on the man's face changed from chubby to dangerous. "I wouldn't talk like that to me, if I were you."

"I don't care how you'd talk to yourself, this is my home and I'm telling you to get out."

"Or what? You'll call the police?"

"I don't need the police." She moved to the door of the kitchen, attempting to go into the living room and open the front door.

The stranger pulled a small pistol from somewhere around his girth and pointed it at her. "I'm actually pretty good with this little thing," he said moving his hand back and forth. "Your water is boiling."

Camille stepped back, feeling those old insecurities returning.

"I said, your water is boiling," he repeated patiently.

After a brief pause, she moved to the stove and picked up the bubbling teakettle, turning off the stovetop. She set it back down, away from the still hot element.

"I told you, I want a cup of tea. It sounds nice." The man's voice was cold steel, his eyes like angry darts. He could do some damage, and Camille knew it. But suddenly her confidence found its way back and she stood her ground.

"You want tea? Make it yourself." She sat down at the kitchen table. He wanted something from her, and she knew he wouldn't kill her until he felt like he'd gotten it. One thing she knew for sure; this man fully intended to get what he'd come for.

Chapter Twenty-Three

"Surely you must want something more than a cup of tea. Are you going to tell me what that is, or should we just enjoy a cup and call it a day?"

"I think you know what I want."

"Oh, right," she said with thick sarcasm. "Like I'd know what some stranger who broke into my house wants from me. Yeah, that works for me. Well, let me think. I haven't been grocery shopping for a few days, and the milk is probably sour, but you're certainly welcome to anything else in the refrigerator that might still be good. Though I think you hardly need it." She glanced at his large stomach.

"You're kind of a smart mouth, now, aren't you?"

Camille smiled sweetly. "Oh, I do try."

The man lunged at her with surprising quickness for his girth, hitting her across the face with the side of his pistol. Camille flew off the chair, banging her head on the wall. "Get up!" he yelled.

She tasted blood as she glared up at the man, getting her feet underneath her and standing, leaning against the wall for support. "Who are you? What do you want?"

"I want the documents your father gave you." His voice was level and sure.

Camille smirked and spat out a rye laugh. "Well, my chubby friend, I'm afraid that ship has sailed. I believe those documents are in the hands of the FBI, or DIN or NAS or some such acronym. I turned them over to the authorities several days ago, at least the pages that weren't blown to tiny little bits in that explosion at the bank."

The man lunged at her again and she shoved him back with both hands, preparing herself for a nice kick to his groin.

He lifted his gun, aiming for her face. "Tell me what they said."

"What they said? The documents? Are you crazy? They were in code! I have no idea what they said. The page that could have decrypted it was in the safe deposit vault and was blown to tiny bits when that vault was robbed." She pulled a napkin from the holder on the table and wiped the blood from her mouth. "That's why they went to the experts. So they could be decrypted."

"Yeah, I used a bit too much explosive on that, didn't I?" He continued without a break, and his next words shocked her to the core. "I shot that Marine too soon. I should have gotten what I needed first."

"You *what?*" Camille took a quick step toward him and he held his aim steady. "You murdered my friend? My boss? No way, that was done by a professional hitman. You're dreaming."

"Maybe it's you who are dreaming. Your 'boyfriend' is FBI, did you know that?"

"Yes, I do know that. And he's not my boyfriend."

Anger welled up inside her as she thought of Tug. He'd sacrificed himself to protect her, as a promise to her mother. She didn't have to wonder if that was true, she knew it was. And standing before her now was the man who'd taken his life from him, and in so doing, had taken his life from her, as well.

"I see. So you read personal notes like the one he left for you and you hug them to you because…why? You like their handwriting?" Camille ignored the comment and the man continued, thinking out loud.

"I'll bet he could help me get those documents back. It might not be too late. If that idiot Naples had done his job, I wouldn't be here now. I've always said, if you want a job done right you'd better do it yourself."

"Who *are* you?"

"I'm a very rich man, and I intend to stay that way."

The man motioned with his gun for Camille to go into the living room. "Go close all the curtains. NOW!"

The stranger, who had initially appeared so very nonthreatening, was becoming agitated and aggressive. His face was suddenly set in stone, his eyes like steel. Camille did as he said and he stayed where he could see her. Once all the curtains were drawn, she turned and waited to see what he wanted her to do.

"Sit down, on the couch and don't move. I obviously don't need you at this point, so if you make me angry, you'll die. I suggest you clean up your attitude. I might just shoot you because I don't really like you, anyway. Too mouthy for me."

Camille said nothing and came around the couch. She sat down slowly and picked up a magazine from her end table. She began perusing it casually, paying no attention to the intruder.

"I think you're mistaken about not needing me, you know." Her eyes never left the magazine.

"Really. And how's that?"

"Well, if my 'boyfriend' can help you, keeping me alive may make him more eager to oblige."

"Look at you being the negotiator. Impressive. Call him. Now."

Camille scanned the room for her purse. He'd taken the bait. "My phone is in my purse. I must have left it with my luggage."

"Stay put. I'll get it for you. Move and you're a dead woman."

"Is it okay if I turn the page?"

He ignored her comment, and after checking her purse for a weapon, tossed it on the couch beside her. She reached inside and pulled out the cell phone.

She began scanning through the list of recent calls. "I don't know his number. I'm sure I have it in my calls list. I'm checking."

Paying no attention to her, he went to the side of the window, lifting the curtain carefully with the barrel of his gun and checking the street in front of the house.

"Here it is. What do you want me to tell him?"

"Thank him for cleaning up your house, invite him over for some tea. Insist that he come. He'll come."

"How did you-"

"I read it before you got here, duh. Now call him. You say one thing that I don't like and I'll kill you where you sit. That would leave a nasty stain on that pretty couch, too."

The smile on his face was as cold as his eyes. He *wanted* to kill her; she could see it in the set of his mouth and she knew he meant what he said. Camille knew if Tope came to her house, he would end up dead. She couldn't risk that. She dialed all but the last digit and waited. When the appropriate amount of time passed, she acted like she was leaving him a message.

"Hey Tope. I really appreciate you taking care of the mess at my place. Thanks so much. Can you get away and have a late lunch with me? Give me a call."

She 'ended' the phony call as Tope and Sawyer screeched to a halt in front of her house.

"That was fast," smiled the intruder. "He must be hungry."

He motioned for Camille to stand and gave her instructions for answering the door. "You're going to open the door enough for him to come in. If you act nervous or try to warn him in any way, I'll kill you both."

Camille nodded, unsure how she was going to get around this. She couldn't let anything happen to Tope.

Footsteps hammered up the front porch. Sawyer must be with him.

"Camille!" Tope pounded on the door. "Camille! Are you in there?"

Camille took a deep breath and opened the door. "What's the hurry? Is something wrong?"

Tope was visibly relieved to see her. "Are you okay?" Tope stepped inside the door and everything happened at once. There was a gunshot and Camille screamed, as the intruder's gun hit Tope on the back of the head. He fell to the floor, unconscious.

Chapter Twenty-Four

Tope floated in blackness, words echoing around him. He couldn't make out any of them, but it was possibly a woman's voice and a very angry man. Tope had been having a very weird dream, something about Henry Fitsimmons but he didn't look the same as the guy at the bank. Well, the same, but different. Really, really different. It almost made Tope laugh.

However, some of his hallucination or dream seemed awfully real. His face was swollen, he could tell, and as he tried to bring himself to full consciousness the words and the voices became clearer, along with his memory. They were no longer in Camille's house, he could tell that. Wherever they were, it didn't smell like Camille's. It didn't smell bad, it just didn't smell like Camille's home.

Henry Fitsimmons had beaten him, wanting…wanting information…to…to know where something was. It was all still very fuzzy, but becoming clearer. Henry Fitsimmons had beaten him? Come on. Impossible. It had to be a dream. But if not Henry, then what caused the swelling of his face?

Tope's head was hanging uncomfortably off the back of the chair and he slowly lifted it. He'd been hit like this before and he knew the outcome. Coming to would be painful and the movement of his head confirmed that fact. He opened the one eye that would work correctly and as light entered his brain he felt like a freight train was seeking entry into his head. He clamped his eye down again and continued to raise his head. As he did, he could feel someone standing in front of him.

"Well look here. Sleeping Beauty awakes. How's the brain, big man? Can you think at all? Because if you can, I want some answers." The voice belonged to Henry Fitsimmons. Tope was certain of it.

"Henry?" Slowly opening one eye, he endured the initial pain. Even still, a soft moan escaped his lips. "Henry Fitsimmons?"

"Yeah, surprise! It's me, and I want those documents. Where are they?"

"Hold up, let me think," said Tope, slowly blinking his good eye. "What documents are you talking about? Why am I supposed to have them?"

"Don't make me hit you again, Daniels. I want the documents you got from Tug Carlson's office. I know he had them. Tug and I had a conversation. He had them alright, but he wasn't willing to share, so I killed him."

Tope tried to process what he was hearing, but it made no sense. "Not possible. Tug's death was a hit."

"Yeah, it was a hit. And I did it. Now tell me what I want to know."

"Clyde Naples did it." Tope couldn't make sense of what he was hearing. The things Henry was telling him didn't fit in with the Henry Tope knew.

"No, Clyde Naples worked for me. I wanted to make sure if Tug went down we would be able to acquire the documents I needed. When Naples assured me he could get them from either your girlfriend, or Tug's girlfriend, I killed Carlson. Not bad for an old guy, yeah?"

"Naples…Naples worked for you? Who are you?"

"My name isn't Henry Fitsimmons, that's for sure. And all you need to know is, I want those documents. I've killed two people to get to them and I'm not afraid to keep going until I get what I want. Now where are they?" Fitsimmons voice grew more agitated with each word.

"Okay, there's something a little off about your story, Henry. A real hitman, a real 'businessman' trading in military secrets would not make this big an error. Right? I mean, those documents are long gone, at the NSA for almost a week now, decrypted and harmless. They were plans for secret military equipment from World War II…obsolete and useless. Surely you would have known that."

Henry barely stopped himself from hitting Tope again. The scream that escaped his mouth was sheer and utter frustration and his feet stomped the floor beneath him. "She wasn't lying. She told me the same thing you're saying. Naples *lied* to me. He had to be working for someone else as well as me. He double crossed me, and if I could kill him again, I would!"

"She? What she? Who are you talking about?"

"Your little girlfriend. Camille. Yeah, I've got her tucked away nice and tight. Looks like you're both going to die today."

Tope tried to force himself to remember how he came to be where he was. The last thing he remembered was arriving with Sawyer at Camille's home. He couldn't even remember getting out of the car, but Sawyer was with him. Saw-

"Where's my partner? Where's Sawyer?" Tope's arms and legs filled with strength fueled by anger. He tried to stand, but found he was bound hand and foot to the chair he was sitting in.

"Oh, that other guy who was with you? Yeah, I remember him from the bank. What a loser. He went down like a rock in pond water. Maybe your memory will improve if I get your little lady out here. She's going to go first, you know, unless you can figure out a way to get me those documents. I might be able to salvage some of this yet. I'll be right back."

The only good part of this situation that he could see was that Camille was still alive. *He said he dropped Sawyer. Could that be true? Sawyer? What would happen to Esley and little Jack? What condition was Camille in? Had she been treated the same as he had?*

The scraping of feet being drug across wood floors interrupted Tope's thoughts. *Where am I anyway*? He tried a quick survey of his surroundings, but his brain wouldn't work that fast just yet. A chair was set down in front of him and Camille was forced into it.

"What have you done to him? Tope, Tope? Can you hear me?"

Fitsimmons secured Camille to the chair as he spoke. "He'll be fine, stop pampering him. He's FBI. He's been through worse than this I'm sure." Addressing Tope he continued. "Can you see who this is, Mr. FBI? It's your lady, and her brains are going to decorate that wall over there if you don't tell me what I want to hear."

Hearing the fear in Camille's voice made him want to tear Fitsimmons' head off. The anger in him was rising, but he knew if he didn't at least pretend to give the man what he wanted, he and Camille would both die. He had to play this out long enough to figure out what he was going to do.

"Okay, okay, what do you want to hear?"

"I want to hear you tell me there is still a way for me to get those documents. I want you to tell me how you're going to make that happen."

"Okay, I will, but first tell me if you killed my partner."

"No, I didn't kill your little friend. He'll live. I'm not stupid enough to kill a police officer or detective or whatever he is." Fitsimmons sighed. "Here's what I'll do for you because I'm such a good guy. I'm gonna give you some time to figure out how you're gonna go about getting me those docs. I don't want to hear it can't be done; I don't want to hear all the *reasons* it can't be done. Just figure it out. I'll be back when I feel like you've had sufficient time to give me a plan."

Fitsimmons turned and left through the back of the house, closing and locking the door behind him.

"Camille, are you okay? Did he hurt you?"

"No, no, I'm fine, but you look awful. Does it hurt much?"

"Not bad. Did you see Sawyer? Is Fitsimmons telling the truth?"

"I saw him go down, but it looked like the bullet just grazed his head. Fitsimmons carried you here over his shoulder with a gun on me. When we got here he tied me up and you started coming around. He started hitting you and hitting you, screaming that he wanted the documents. I couldn't stop him – I couldn't get free."

"It's not your fault, Camille. I'll be fine." Tope knew if he looked anything like how he felt, she would know that last part was a guess. "He carried me over his shoulder? He's stronger than he looks. Where are we?" Tope was having a hard time seeing his surroundings.

"You're not going to believe where we are. We're about two doors down from my house. He drove for about an hour and a half with you unconscious and me blindfolded in the back of a paneled van. He thought he was being so clever, but the neighbor on the other side of me has a very large dog that barks into all hours of the night. I've listened to that dog long enough to know exactly where we are. This guy's an idiot."

"I think it's more like you're amazingly smart. Most people in this situation wouldn't stay calm enough to recognize that. You did great." Tope was working the ropes that held his hands. He lowered his voice to barely a whisper.

"Can you hear me if I talk this low?"

"I think so," Camille responded as softly.

"He may have a bug in here and could be listening to our conversation. We need to keep talking at the regular volume so he doesn't suspect we know. When we need to communicate anything we hope he won't hear, just whisper like this."

"Okay."

"So," began Tope, speaking freely. "How are we going to get those documents out of the police station? You know Captain Amerson had them in his desk. Do you think they're still there?"

Camille played along. "I don't know. I…I know he had them in there the last time we met. I watched him put them back after we talked."

Using his eye was becoming less and less painful as he became accustomed to the light in the room. "Do you know what time it is?"

"It's late, I know that much. If the clock on the wall is correct, it's about midnight."

Tope whispered again. "I'm going to try to move my chair. Talk to me; think of something to say that will take a while to explain. Anything. Make up a horrendous lie. Just keep talking so you can hopefully mask the noise of my movements." He began forcing the chair to move with jerks of his body. The sound was very loud, the pain excruciating, but it couldn't be helped. Every movement sent pain shooting everywhere. He had no idea what hurt and why, but he had to make this work.

Camille started right in. "You know, Tope, we may not make it out of this alive and I really feel like I need to tell you exactly how I feel about you. I love you. I think you're the most amazing man I've ever known."

As the words poured from Camille's mouth, Tope tried not to think about what she was saying. He'd told her to make up a lie. Was she lying? He couldn't allow himself to think about that right now. He attempted to stand, and his ribs screamed pain throughout his whole body. He sat back trying to breath.

"I…I hear you Camille. I guess we should have had this talk weeks ago."

He motioned to her with his head to keep talking.

"Yes, but I'd been through so much, losing Tug and the protection he offered me. Did I ever tell you about the time…" Camille continued with a story that would clearly take some time to complete. She was amazing at this.

Tope interjected words every once in a while to indicate he was listening to her. He was able to move his chair until it was nearly beside Camille's. If he could position his chair behind hers, he may be able to loosen her bindings enough for her to wriggle free.

He was about there, just a few more hops and the back door opened. Camille stopped her story midsentence and sat quietly.

Henry Fitsimmons strolled into the room and dropped his keys into a bowl on the kitchen table. He approached Tope and grabbing his hair, yanked his head back so hard, Tope thought it was going to come right off his neck.

"Motion sensors, idiot," spat Fitsimmons. "Yeah, and really, really sensitive bugs on the bottom of your chair." He put his face down inches from Tope's and whispered. "I heard every word."

He released Tope's head with a jerk that sent the room spinning. Tope forced a smile and said offhandedly, "You can't blame a guy for trying, can you? I had to know if you were listening in. Now that I know, I can focus on what it is you want."

"Too late. I don't have any more time to waste. Looks like one of you is going to die. Such a beautiful couple, too. A shame, really. But necessary."

Fitsimmons slowly walked around the two chairs, eyeing each of his prisoners with the cold steel eyes of a killer. "So, which one will it be?"

Chapter Twenty-Five

Sawyer floated in and out of consciousness, occasionally hearing the ambulance sirens and voices around him. Often he felt weightless, hovering over his family, watching them and wanting to hold them in his arms.

When he finally returned to full consciousness, two days had passed. As he woke, he saw Esley seated in the chair beside his hospital bed, sound asleep, drool running from the corner of her mouth. The sight made him smile and he squeezed her hand. She jumped at the touch and wiped her mouth as she sat forward.

"You were drooling again," he said, trying not to laugh. It seemed even the sound of his own voice caused pain in his head that made him want to lose his stomach contents.

"You *would* notice that first," she teased. Then glancing to Sawyer's bandaged head, she sobered. "I can only say it's a good thing I'm not a police officer anymore. That guy would be dead."

"What guy?"

"What do you remember?"

Sawyer scowled, trying to bring back the events prior to the...to the... He tried to focus, to think about where he'd been and what had happened there, but he couldn't remember anything at all.

"I felt like I was in space, a big empty black void. I can't remember anything."

"Do you remember driving to Camille's house?"

"Camille...Camille...I do remember something about that name, but I can't remember why we were going, or... 'we?' I don't know who 'we' is."

"You will. It will all come back to you. For now, you need to rest."

"But what happened to me? Why am I here?"

Esley sat back in her chair. She smiled softly. "That will have to come from the doctor. He's expected in any time. To be honest, I was afraid you wouldn't know who I was."

"Yeah, like that could happen," he said, smiling carefully. He lifted his hand to his head and felt the bandage. "Why does my head hurt so bad? I've got an awful headache."

Dr. Matheson strolled into the room just as Sawyer finished his sentence. "Why does your head hurt so bad? It happens when you go banging your head on porch railings."

"Porch railings?"

The doctor glanced at Esley. "How much does he remember?"

"Hey, Doc, I'm right here. I remember floating in blackness, and getting up a little early this morning to play with my son before I left for work. I let Esley sleep a little longer."

Esley searched her husband's face, at a loss for how to tell him the facts. "Sawyer," she said squeezing his hand, "that was two days ago."

"What?" His face took on a stunned look and his eyes traveled from Esley to the doctor. "What is she talking about?"

Dr. Matheson spoke calmly. "You were shot, Sawyer, and you were incredibly lucky. The bullet grazed your left arm, but your head hit the railing on the porch when you fell back. You sustained what's called a closed, or simple fracture in that fall. You'll probably have a short time where you can't remember the incident, but it will come back eventually. We're going to keep you here for a couple of days.

"A word, Mrs. Kingsley?" he nodded to the hall.

Esley followed the doctor, her face anxious. Dr. Matheson stopped just outside the door and turned to face her.

"I think it's best not to tell him of the two individuals who are missing. We don't want to force his memory. He will remember in time, and when he asks about them, you can tell him what you know, but nothing that he doesn't ask for. Okay?"

"Yes, nothing he doesn't ask for," Esley nodded, her dark eyes wide.

"Don't be afraid, Mrs. Kingsley. He's going to be just fine. I'd be willing to bet, by the time he goes home his memory will be completely restored. No need to worry."

He smiled kindly and was hurrying down the hallway to his next appointment. Esley watched him walk away as tears filled her eyes. Her fear of losing Sawyer had weighed heavily on her. The fact that it took two days for him to wake scared her more than she could even explain to anyone. She looked longingly at the doctor, wishing she could dismiss all these feelings as he had when he walked away.

Esley returned to Sawyer's room, composed, with tears dried. She sat down in her chair.

"I ordered your food for you, hope you like it. I've been thoroughly enjoying your meals, since you were sleeping." She smiled broadly.

"Something is missing. Something isn't right about all of this. I feel like I need to be someplace else, doing something else."

"Don't do this Sawyer. You're right where you need to be, doing what you need to be doing, getting better. You need to rest."

"When can I go home? How is Jack? Who is watching him?"

"He's at the neighbor's playing with their son. Those two are going to grow up to be best friends, for sure. He just squeals when I drop him off. It's so cute. He misses you, but I told him you would be home soon."

Sawyer's eyelids drooped and he laid his head back against the pillow. Knowing if she instructed him to sleep he wouldn't do it, she took another route.

"I'm going to lie down on my chariot over there," she said, stretching and pointing behind her.

"I'm so tired. It's not often I get a nap in the middle of the day, and I'm taking advantage of it."

Sawyer just nodded and closed his eyes. "I know what you're doing, Es, and I love you for it," he murmured as his eyelids fell.

❖❖❖

Sawyer was in a large open space with a table and two chairs in the center of it. The only light source was directly overhead and shone down creating a small, lighted area. Sawyer sat in one chair and Jack sat in the other. It was no surprise to see his old partner; it was just as it should be. They visited about cases they'd worked in the past, and joked about some of their favorite perps.

"Remember that old lady," chuckled Jack, "who would shove her ratty old cat up into the tree in her backyard just so she could have you come and get it out for her? She had the *hots* for you."

"I think it was really you she was after," said Sawyer, laughing. "She even said you had 'such a nice butt.' " The memory made him laugh even harder.

"She had to be in her early nineties, didn't she?" laughed Jack. "I guess she just knew a good thing when she saw it."

The laughter died down and Sawyer stared into Jack's eyes. "This is wrong. You're not supposed to be here."

"No, not exactly, depending on where you think 'here' is. Maybe it's *you* who are not supposed to be *here*."

Sawyer's head spun and Jack was suddenly gone, replaced with Tope, different, yet the same as his old partner. "Are you Jack?" Sawyer was certain there was enough difference to know this wasn't the same person, and yet the resemblance was striking.

"No, Sawyer. My name is Tope. I'm your new partner, remember? My name is Tope. I'm Jack's nephew. We look a lot alike, I know. Can be kind of confusing. But, I'm not Jack. Jack died. Do you remember that?"

The room spun again and this time Sawyer was certain it was Jack Baker in the chair.

"You have to help Tope, Sawyer. He's in danger, and if you don't find him very soon, he will die. I'm here telling you this because he needs you to find him. Find him, Sawyer. Find Tope."

The rooms spun yet again, and this time Sawyer floated over his family, Esley and baby Jack. Baby Jack, named for his dear friend. His friend and brother, Jack Baker who had a…a…nephew. He had a nephew…and his name was…

"TOPE!!"

Esley jumped when Sawyer screamed his partner's name. He'd awoken agitated and angry, the ache in his head apparently not as strong as it was before. Esley tried to calm him down but he wouldn't listen to her.

"Sawyer, you have to calm down. You have to stay where you are for now. I'll tell the captain, Sawyer, I promise you. I'll get Jack's message to Captain Amerson. He'll find Tope, Sawyer. The captain will find Tope."

"I have to find him. Jack says Tope will die if I don't find him. I have to go find him."

Esley rang for the nurse who came in and saw Sawyer's state of mind. She quickly ran and got a sedative.

Sawyer saw her come back in with the syringe and his eyes grew wide with anger and frustration.

"NO! NO! I have to get up. Esley, don't let her shoot me with that, I have to find Tope. He's out there and I have to find him. Jack is depending on me."

The injection went into the IV line and within moments Sawyer's screams were reduced to panicked whispers and soon he was out completely.

"Thank you," sighed Esley. "I didn't know what to do."

"You did the right thing," said the nurse, smiling softly. "He needs rest. You may as well go home now. He'll sleep the whole night."

Esley stood, unwilling to leave her husband again and go home to a house with just her and Jack in it. In her heart she knew Sawyer would be fine, but his absence made their home far too big. She missed him. Jack missed him. She wanted him to come home.

Chapter Twenty-Six

For the last two days, Fitsimmons had threatened Tope and Camille that one of them would die if they didn't come up with the documents. He would stroll casually around their two chairs and stop randomly at one, lift his gun to his prisoner's head, and pulled the trigger. He told them there was a single bullet in the chamber, but that he didn't know which pull of the trigger would force it from its place.

The first several times, when the gun was pointed at Camille's head, Tope had pleaded with Fitsimmons to listen to him, that he had a way to get the documents back from the NSA, but the evil smile would slide across Fitsimmons' face as he pulled the trigger. The gun never fired, and either the man couldn't count, or he had no intention of killing either of them because in the two days of playing his little game, the chamber had already made several complete rotations and no bullet was ever fired. The man was cruel and sadistic.

Several interesting things about Fitsimmons had come out in their conversations over the days, helping Tope to understand some details about the man and his life. The training he'd had in the service had backfired with Fitsimmons. Instead of hating what he had to do and hating the killing he was training for as a sniper, he relished in it. He delighted in every kill, in the shocked and stunned faces of those who witnessed it. He'd quickly become every trainer's nightmare.

Apparently this was recognized early on in his career, and something happened that caused Fitsimmons to be dishonorably discharged. He wouldn't elaborate on the story, but he became very angry when Tope pressed him about it.

This man, Henry Fitsimmons, was clearly crazy, and that insanity made him doubly dangerous. Tope had to get Camille out of this situation and he had to do it quickly. A man in Fitsimmons' condition usually tired of his sadistic games and ended the whole affair. But whatever he thought was in those documents, drove him beyond his usual limit of patience. That was a lucky break for Tope and Camille.

The swelling of Tope's face had gone down quite a bit, and Fitsimmons had thrown no more punches since their initial capture. He was now able to see clearly and often scanned the room for anything useful for a successful escape.

Tope had also kept his fingers moving whenever Fitsimmons wasn't aware to keep the swelling in his arms and wrists to a minimum. It was all about blood flow, and if he could work the bindings that held his arms behind the chair, he might be able to loosen the ropes and get free, assuming he could be successful in keeping the swelling down. He'd been working the knots every chance he got and he thought he felt some wiggle room. Not enough to get out of them yet, but soon.

Fitsimmons was gone for longer periods of time now, but Camille and Tope knew to be quiet. They said nothing, and didn't try to move their chairs, but sent soundless words back and forth, some understood, but mostly not. It was frustrating to both of them, but they had to keep trying.

Tope didn't believe Fitsimmons had motion sensors set up, he was certain he'd see them if they were there. The listening devices were more believable. Still, Tope was hesitant to try moving again, just in case Fitsimmons wasn't lying about the motion sensors. He tried tipping his chair just a little bit, and there was no response from Fitsimmons. There were no cameras present, that Tope could see, and as Tope was becoming more and more desperate to get free, he decided he'd risk movement.

Gradually at first, he scooted his chair a fraction of an inch toward Camille. Tope's teeth scraped against each other in an effort to keep the groans of pain inside him. Camille's eyes grew wide with fear and she shook her head adamantly, motioning with her head for him to stop.

No response from Fitsimmons. Not knowing how far away he actually was, whether or not he knew there was movement in the house, and how soon it would be before he returned, Tope made his move.

Ignoring the screaming pain, he scooted his chair slowly around Camille's until they were back to back. He worked furiously at the knots that held her, knowing that the movement of his chair had been less than quiet. If Fitsimmons were where he could hear and be aware of the noise, he would be on his way back to the house right now, if he'd even left it. If he hadn't left the house and was in the garage or the yard, or even sitting in the car outside, they were toast and he knew it.

After several minutes of work, Camille's hands were free. She bent over and untied her feet and stood for the first time in nearly three days. Her legs and arms screamed at the sudden movement, but she ignored them and moved her chair aside as quietly as she could. She'd no sooner begun to release Tope's bindings then that familiar voice came from behind.

"So, you want to die first, eh, Camille?"

His tone was sleazy, slippery, like oil on water. In a second he was on her and holding her neck, forcing her to move forward as they stumbled around to where Tope could see them.

Tope's covert ops training kicked into high gear and he remained calm, keeping his eyes focused like steel tipped arrows on Fitsimmons, not looking at his hostage.

"You don't want to do this, Henry, you're just going to make more trouble for yourself and that's not going to be good."

"Where are the documents? You're lying about the NSA; you didn't send them there. Why would you? You're keeping them for yourself. You're not fooling me for an instant. They're a gold mine and you know it. There are countries who will offer top dollar for that information."

"What makes you say that? The NSA has already gotten back with us. The information in the decrypted documents is obsolete. You have to know that. This whole thing has done you no good at all. Let her go, release me, and we'll all walk away."

"No can do. I'm not going to give up on this. I *know* there has to be more to them than 'obsolete information.' I've been offered a great deal of money for what's on those pages, by a country who's good for the payment, and I intend to collect every penny."

Tope smiled carefully, making sure his facial expressions didn't portray mockery. "I can see you've thought this out very carefully. But you need to listen to me. I'm trying to tell you the truth. Camillè brought us the documents, minus the stolen decryption code, and we had to send them to the best decryption department in the country, the NSA, and they decoded it."

"There *was* no decryption code, you moron!" Fitsimmons was beginning to breathe heavily; beads of sweat formed on his high forehead.

Camille remained calm, and if anything appeared to be growing angry, which probably wasn't a good thing. Tope was hoping his own calm demeanor might transfer to Camille and help her understand he had everything under control. He hoped she could hang in there for a while longer.

"Henry, someone stole the decryption code from the safe deposit vault, remember? It exploded."

"Don't patronize me, you fool! I blew up that vault, I broke into the drawer that Tug had rented and it was empty. The rental of the safe deposit box was a ruse. That's why I killed him. He was no good to me if he didn't have the decryption code and if he didn't have that, then I was certain Little Miss, here, was the one with the coded documents *and* the decryption codes. She'd made it look like she'd given them to Tug, but in reality, she didn't. So I hired Naples."

"*You* hired Naples?" Tope was surprised at the information.

"*YES*, I hired Naples!" Spittle flew from him mouth as he screamed the words. "You're wasting my time! I want those documents and Camille here is going to show me where they are."

By now, the look on Camille's face was pure irritation.

"Oh, for crying out loud," she moaned. "This has gone on long enough."

Camille bent forward and reached back, into Fitsimmons groin. She growled, grabbing a handful of soft flesh and squeezed with all her might. "Look what you did to his beautiful face!" she cried, motioning to Tope. "If it stays that way, I'll make you sorry your parents ever had that first date!"

Fitsimmons bent over in pain and Camille turned to face him.

"And you kept us tied up for three days! *YOU* are the moron, and you're gonna pay. I can't stand to listen to your voice for one more second!"

As those last words flew from her mouth, she lifted her knee and bashed his head against it in one swift move. Her attacker began to fall and his gun dropped to the floor. When he hit the floor, writhing in pain, Camille kicked the gun away from him and with something of a growl mixed with a scream, she took her foot and stomped on his crotch.

"And *THAT* is for calling me 'Little Miss,' you *jackass*!"

Fitsimmons screamed in pain.

"Man that felt good! What a weasel." Camille ran to Tope and quickly untied his already loosened rope. She helped him out of his chair and headed for the door.

"Grab his gun! Grab his gun!" yelled Tope, holding his ribcage. Camille turned, grabbed the gun, and the two of them hurried out the back door.

"Where did you learn to do that? *Very* impressive!" Tope was speaking through gritted teeth, but he couldn't help being astonished by her actions.

Camille was busy watching behind them for signs of their captor, but Fitsimmons was obviously still in the house. "We don't have long, but we need to find somewhere to hide."

They approached the street and saw Tope's car still parked at the curb in front of Camille's home. "Help me get to the car. I keep a spare key in the wheel well. We have to hurry!"

"We can just hide in my house, can't we?" Camille gaped anxiously at Tope.

"He got in there once, didn't he? We have to assume he can get in there again. Just get the key from the driver's side wheel well! You'll have to drive."

"Okay, okay."

Tope limped to the passenger side of the car. Camille reached into the wheel well and felt around until she found a small box. She grabbed the box and pulled. The small box came off easily in her hand and she slid the top open, grabbed the spare key and dropped the box on the pavement. Just as she'd pulled the keys from the box, she started for the door and looked up to see Fitsimmons racing around the side of the house, heading right for them, straight down the sidewalk. The man was definitely faster than he looked.

Chapter Twenty-Seven

Tope had also had enough. Adrenalin pumped through his veins and he stood on the sidewalk waiting for Fitsimmons to get to him. The attacker slowed and eyed both of them with cautiously cunning eyes.

Camille held his gun pointed right at him. "I'm pretty good with a gun, *Little Man*, but if you want to test me out, just take one more step so I can blow your head off with a smile on my face. My father was a pretty good shot. We went shooting every weekend. I liked it, a lot."

Tope didn't wait for Fitsimmons to attack. Instead, he ignored his raging ribcage and kicked Fitsimmons in the stomach, throwing him back against Camille's picket fence. The fence cracked and popped, breaking under the weight as the man flew onto his back across her flowerbed. Broken pieces of fencing lay around him like oversized Popsicle sticks.

Knowing he'd reached the limit of what his body was going to give him, Tope yelled to Camille, "Get in the car, *NOW!*"

Camille quickly slipped the key in the lock and turned it, opening the door and manually unlocking Tope's door. Just as they were about to slide into the front seats, three police cruisers and an ambulance came screaming around the corner. They pulled up in front of Camille's house with guns drawn on poor Mr. Fitsimmons, who was now trying to get himself out of the flowerbed with some sense of decorum. It wasn't happening.

Eventually, Fitsimmons dropped his head back onto the ground and his hands fell to his sides. Tope leaned forward against the side of the car, resting his arm on the roof of the car and dropping his head onto his arm.

Captain Amerson came in behind the ambulance and pulled in front of Tope's car, jumping from the driver's seat and running to Camille without pausing to close his car door. He put his hand on her shoulder but she shook her head and motioned to Tope. "Please, help Tope. He's hurt bad." Worry was evident in her tear filled eyes. She followed the captain around the car as he headed toward Tope.

"I need paramedics over here, now! Bring a gurney!" The captain called out instructions when he saw Tope barely able to stand. Captain Amerson put Tope's arm around his neck and grabbed his hand, pulling it gently. Holding his other arm around Tope's shoulder, Amerson helped Tope step back from the car. Tope's breathing was shallow and he was growing weaker by the minute.

Camille was instantly at his side. "Tope, Tope, I'm here," she whispered softly into his ear. "I always will be, Tope. Always. Just don't leave me or I swear I'll shoot you myself."

As they laid Tope onto the gurney, he forced his eyes to focus on Camille. "You're a feisty little miss, aren't you?" He grinned softly.

"Call me that again and I'll give you a dose of what I gave Fitsimmons, don't forget it."

"Sorry," he smiled softly. "I had to see how it felt."

Camille laughed as the tears rolled freely down her cheeks. "I'm taking your car to the hospital. And I'm not asking you, I'm telling you."

❖❖❖

Tope woke to soft music and Camille sitting by his bed quietly reading a book.

"We've got to stop meeting like this," he said. "People will talk."

"Yeah? Let them talk, I say. A little speculation never hurt anyone."

He cocked his head and frowned slightly. "Have you even been home? How long have I been in here?"

Camille checked her watch. "Four hours, six minutes, twenty-nine seconds."

"Wow, you like to be exact."

"Yes I do."

"Have we gotten any word on how Sawyer is doing?"

Camille set the book in her lap and put the bookmark in it before slowly closing it. "Yeah, but it's not real good."

"What do you mean? What does 'not real good' mean?"

"I spoke with Esley just after you were brought in and Sawyer only remembered you and I in the twenty-four hours he was here. The doctor said as the swelling around his brain goes down, his memory will improve, but it's going to take some time."

"His brain? What happened to his brain?"

"Evidently, he banged his head on my porch railing when he was shot by Fitsimmons and cracked his skull. It's not uncommon in injuries like that to have a temporary memory lapse. It's only been three days since he fell. It will take some time."

"Well...can we see him? I'd like to go see him. Where is his room? Is he on this floor?"

Camille stood and touched Tope's shoulder, letting him know he was staying put. She leaned over and kissed his forehead.

"*You* are staying put," she said firmly. "I have been checking on him, and bits and pieces of the night it happened are coming back to him. As for you, you broke two ribs, and one of them nearly pierced your heart. You are laying low for several weeks, whether you like it or not. At least until that rogue rib decides to stop complaining and heal."

Tope winced from the movement and settled into his pillow. "You're a hard one, you know. I always thought you needed someone to take care of you. Now I'm beginning to think you want someone to take care of." He smiled and his eyes focused on hers, staring into her soul.

"Stop that." Camille shifted her blouse, smoothing it down the front.

"Stop what?"

"Stop staring at me."

"Stop making me stare."

Camille sighed. "Captain Amerson told me if you gave me any grief I was to call him and he would be here in a matter of minutes. Do you want me to call Captain Amerson? Don't think I won't, mister."

Tope didn't dare laugh, but it was hard not to. He'd found a woman who was not only smart, but also fully able to take care of herself. Life might be fun after all.

❖❖❖

Summer was in full bloom and the days were becoming warmer. Esley hugged Jack and kissed his forehead, thanking the neighbor for her help while Esley was at the hospital with Sawyer.

Esley knew the sense of relief that comes with having a case near closing. Fitsimmons was in lockup, where he definitely belonged from the sound of things, and the other man, Naples, was dead. She was happy to be home with an ever changing, always growing, little human being who directed her life in appreciation of humanity, instead of death and criminals.

Pulling into the hospital parking lot, she saw Captain Amerson getting out of his car. She parked, grabbed her purse, and hurried to catch up with him.

"Hey Captain! You must be feeling pretty good about things." Esley spoke as she came up behind him.

"I guess I'd be feeling better if my two top investigators weren't in the hospital," he replied, shaking his head. "This has been a hard one. Jack's death was emotionally difficult, probably the hardest thing Sawyer has ever been through. But this one...*this* one has been more physically difficult than any other case we've ever had. I don't remember the last time I've had the same guys in the hospital this many times." The captain thought for a moment. "But, yes, it's good to be done with. Far as I'm concerned, Mr. Fitsimmons can rot in lock up for as long as it takes Sawyer and Tope to recuperate."

"I doubt the legal system will allow that," scoffed Esley.

"We've got some tricks up our sleeve if we need it. For now, I just want them to focus on getting better. How is Sawyer? I'm just on my way to see him."

"His memory is coming back, but it's a lot slower than the doctors thought it would be. Sometimes..." Esley's voice trailed off and she went silent.

"Sometimes what?"

"Oh, it's probably stupid. I'm not a psychologist, but I can't help but wonder if some of his memory loss is psychological. I mean, Jack Baker's death was so hard for him, and in some ways he's still dealing with that loss. The thought of losing Tope, who is so much like Jack, well...I just think it's easier to forget than to deal with. You know?"

"That's pretty good reasoning, I'd say, considering I was talking with Maizy, our department psychologist, just a few minutes ago and she said pretty much the same thing. She's been in to see Sawyer and he didn't recognize her at all. That was last week, so that may have changed."

"Let's hope so."

The hospital doors swung open and Esley and Captain Amerson entered the main area and proceeded to the elevators.

Entering Sawyer's hospital room, Esley could see Sawyer's agitation before he even said a word. He was up sitting on the edge of his bed and putting on his slippers.

"Why didn't you tell me Tope was in the hospital? I've been wondering if he and Camille were even alive! Why didn't you tell me?" He stood on legs still a little wobbly, steadying himself with one hand on the bed.

"Sawyer, sit down. I can explain everything, but you're going to have to sit down if you want to hear it."

Captain Amerson helped Esley get Sawyer back into bed, all the while listening to how angry he was that he hadn't been informed of his partner's admittance to the hospital.

Esley and the captain pulled their chairs up to the side of the bed, Esley on one side, the captain on the other. Esley began.

"Sawyer, the doctor told me I was to wait until you asked about Tope or Camille before I tried to talk to you about them. You had a dream about Tope, I know that, but you hadn't remembered Camille, yet. I'm so happy your memory is coming back. Can you remember the incident?"

Sawyer was angry and still agitated. He was unable to keep his legs still, and he couldn't seem to decide whether his arms should go over his head or at his sides.

"I remember it all, of course I remember it. Why would you ask me that?"

Chapter Twenty-Eight

The doctor had explained days before, that when he began remembering things he might be angry and hard to deal with, but that this, too, would pass in time.

"Sawyer, it's me, Esley. You know I wouldn't hide things from you, you know I wouldn't try to trick you. Your memory is coming back and that can be a little disconcerting. You didn't know how you ended up in the hospital for days, only now are you remembering the incident. You *know* me, Sawyer."

Her words seemed to calm him some, and his body slowly relaxed.

"I know, I know," he said softly. "I…I hate that I can't seem to catch up with my brain. It's feeding me things faster than I can process them, and it makes me mistrust, not just everyone else, but myself as well."

"We were told you'd feel this way. Just try to stay calm and let the memories come. Accept them when they do, don't fight them and try to tell yourself they're not true. Your brain is waking up and it must be frustrating, I'm sure. I love you, Sawyer. You know that, right?"

"I do know that, replied Sawyer, stroking Esley's hand softly and continuing. "How is Baby Jack doing? Is he okay? Is he frightened that I'm not home?"

"Well…he's certainly not happy about it. At his bath each night, before I put him in bed, he asks for Daddy. I tell him you'll be home soon."

Sawyer smiled for the first time that morning. It felt good to see his smile return.

"I'll tell you what." Esley stood and patted his hand. "You visit with Captain Amerson for a minute and I'll ask about a wheelchair to take you to Tope's room."

She turned and left the room and Sawyer saw his captain sitting beside the bed for the first time.

"Hey, Sawyer. When are you going to get off your lazy butt and get back to work?"

Sawyer chuckled. "Yup. It's definitely you. I remember that bossy tone. Believe me, I'm more than ready to hit the streets. Tell me what happened while I was forgetting everything."

Captain Amerson explained to him about Camille and Tope's capture and escape, and that Henry Fitsimmons was now in custody.

"Henry Fitsimmons? The *bank manager*? Are you kidding me? He's a weasel, but he's certainly not a killer."

The captain smiled. "Apparently he is. He admitted to killing Tug and Naples, and to blowing up Naples' hideout. So far he's told us that Naples apparently had that hideout built with his own funds. We've learned that Naples was connected to a private server owned by Fitsimmons and reported directly to Fitsimmons, who hired Naples. Naples was somewhat of a hired gun, it appears."

"I'm trying to picture Fitsimmons as a sniper," he said with a smile. "It's really not working for me."

Captain Amerson chuckled. "We've all had that same problem. Fitsimmons tried to pin Tug's murder on Naples. Problem was, he'd already bragged about killing both Tug and Naples to Camille and Tope when he was holding them prisoner. It's no wonder the military discharged him. He's a menace to himself, not just his country."

"Discharged?" Sawyer looked questioningly at his Captain. "Ever find out why?"

"Something happened to him with his first few kills as a sniper, according to his military records. He tested well with the program and in the beginning, everything seemed to be in order. But either he was a good actor or he had issues that didn't come up in the test. Hard to tell. Either way, he hoped to make a killing on a list of known U.S. operatives. Unaware of the second line of code needed to decrypt the cypher, he'd have had nothing."

Sawyer shook his head in disbelief. "I don't even know how to respond to all that. He seemed like a harmless little nobody, scared of his own shadow. Benign. Definitely benign. He was a great actor."

Esley came through the door with a large grin and a wheelchair. Sawyer was finally going to have a visit with his partner.

Wheeling Sawyer into the room, his face took on a look of utter shock. "J…J…Jack. It's…It's you. You're alive!"

Tope didn't know how to react. Camille stood and took his hand and slowly a look of understanding washed over Sawyer's face.

Esley knelt down beside the wheelchair and looked up in to Sawyer's eyes. "Think back, Sawyer, Jack is gone. Tope came to work with you from Washington, D.C. Do you remember that?"

"Yes, yes, I remember," Sawyer replied, patting Esley's hand. "I'm sorry Tope. My brain was 'in park' for a while and now it seems like it's racing to catch up. I'm good. I hope I didn't scare you with that greeting."

Tope smiled at his partner. "It's great to see you, Sawyer."

"I heard what happened with you and Camille. Are you both alright?"

Camille nodded her head and Tope gazed up at her, softly moving her hand back and forth as he spoke. "We're better than alright. Okay, so, yeah, I've got a little healing to do, but nothing death defying. Just some broken ribs."

"Your face doesn't look so good." Sawyer chuckled. "But then you never were much to look at."

"And here I was hoping I'd get a better version of you out of this whole ordeal. No such luck. Nice."

Captain Amerson had stayed behind Esley and Sawyer, giving the two men some time to connect. He spoke now, relieved to see Sawyer's memory returning, but worried about his detectives. "You boys better get your rest. There's still work to do on this case and I expect you two to be ready to testify in court when the time arises. So no all-night parties in your hospital rooms, you hear?"

Camille laughed. "He'll be coming home with me as soon as he's released. I have a guest room and it will be his new home while he recovers."

Tope looked up at her in surprise. "The *guest* room?"

Camille eyed him firmly. "The *guest* room."

❖❖❖

Several weeks later, Tope and Sawyer sat in an interrogation room with Henry Fitsimmons. They were there to wrap up details of his arrest prior to his court hearing.

Sawyer still had a difficult time wrapping his head around who this plump little man said he was. Tope had no such difficulty. He'd seen this man move, and it still surprised him.

Sawyer started the interview. "We understand, from what you told Tope and Camille, that you were the one who blew up the safe deposit vault. Is that correct?"

Fitsimmons smiled cunningly, his eyes disappearing into the folds of his face as he did. "Yeah, I did that. A little bit of overkill, I guess. I don't have much experience with explosives. I was a sniper."

"And not for very long, I understand," said Tope. "They dumped you after your second op, isn't that right?"

The smug smile was gone, replaced with a venomous glare. "They didn't know what they had. I could have done so much for them."

Tope leaned into the table, resting his forearms on the edge and folding his hands. "My guess is they knew *exactly* what they had, and were happy to get rid of it."

"Calm down," said Sawyer, casting a warning glance at Tope. "How did you get Clyde Naples' name? How did you know about him?"

"I don't have to tell you anything. I'll be my own defense attorney, as you've probably heard, and I'm counseling myself not to say anything."

"No, you don't, but it might go better for you at your trial, if you cooperate." Sawyer leaned back in his chair to let his words sink in.

"You don't have a conviction yet." Fitsimmons eyes narrowed. "And I'm not going to help you convict me. You've got nothing."

Tope couldn't help feeling sorry for Henry Fitsimmons. He truly was an emotionally sick man. He had no idea what he was up against in a court of law, but with Sawyer's help, he was about to find out.

"Nothing, eh?" Sawyer smiled broadly and leaned forward. "Let's see what we've got… There are two counts of murder, both of which you admitted to, you admitted it was you who blew the safety deposit vault at the bank, two counts of kidnapping, one of those is kidnapping a federal agent, breaking and entering, assault on a federal agent, attempted murder of a police officer…shall I continue?"

"Okay, listen," said Fitsimmons, "I've got money. I've got lots of money in offshore accounts, all over the world. You'd never have to work another day in your lives. Just get me out of here and you're home free. We'll all be home free."

Sawyer couldn't wipe the smile off his face. "Oh, and now bribery. You're going down Mr. Fitsimmons. And Tope and I are going to have a front row seat."

The two men rose and left the interrogation room to vile threats and protests from the prisoner. It only served to make the arrest that much sweeter.

❖❖❖

After helping Camille into the passenger seat, Tope came around and slid into the driver's seat.

"What do you say we try that Italian restaurant…what was it…Mario's, right? Maybe this time we'll actually get to eat dinner." He smiled at her and leaned over, kissing her softly. He touched her hair, felt the warmth of her smile, and kissed her again, feeling her lean into him.

"I'm good with that," she said, staring into his eyes like she could read his thoughts. "You do owe me dinner there, you know. After as many dates as we've been on, I thought you'd eventually remember your debt."

"Oh? How do you figure I *owe* you?"

Camille's eyes took on an innocent air. "As I recall, you said we'd definitely, yes, I believe the word was 'definitely,' have to try this again, meaning the restaurant. Your own words."

"If you don't stop doing that, we'll not be having dinner until much later."

"I'm sure I don't know what you mean."

"I'm sure you do." Tope stuck the key in the ignition, turning it quickly, and they headed to the restaurant.

They were seated by the window and presented with menus. Tope knew what he was having right away. "I never did get to try that Lasagna. I'm having that. You?" He raised his eyebrows and dipped his chin at his date.

"I'll have the same."

"And a bottle of your Chianti Classico, as well."

The waiter picked up the menus. "Very good, sir."

The light from the candle on the table danced in Camille's eyes as she studied him across the table. "Finally, we get our night at Mario's. I've wanted to come here since I was twelve."

"Are you telling me you've never eaten here before? I find that hard to believe. What about prom? Didn't guys take their dates to fancy restaurants?"

The waiter returned with the wine and, after Tope nodded his approval, the wine was poured and the waiter left.

"We were farmers. And I never went to prom."

"You're lying." Tope couldn't believe what he was hearing.

"No, I'm not," Camille said, her eyebrows raised. "I didn't have time for boys. I was in charge of our farm animals, and Dad needed me."

"Even on prom night?"

"Even on prom night, and I was happy for the escape."

"Oh, I see. A tomboy."

Camille cocked her head to one side. "I guess you could say that."

The waiter returned with a silver tray bearing a silver cover. With a wink at Tope, he set the tray in front of Camille."

"An appetizer for the lady."

Camille's eyes widened and she looked over the tall cover to where Tope was sitting, his grin almost reaching to the sides of his face.

"What is *this*?"

"Oh, something I thought you might like."

She lifted the lid and gasped. Sitting atop a large bed of green lettuce was a small red velvet box.

"What. Is. This?"

"I bought you a cake," replied Tope with a wink. "Open it and see."

Camille shook as she opened the box. Tears filled her eyes and she set the box back down on the tray and covered her mouth with both hands.

Tope stood and came around to Camille's chair. Taking the box from the tray, he knelt down on one knee and the restaurant fell silent.

"Camille Cofford, I ask you on this most special night, with my heart as open as this box, will you marry me?"

The two stood and Tope put his arms around her waist. She gently placed her hands on the back of his head, and with eyes filled with tearful delight that flowed effortlessly down her face, she nodded in the affirmative. "Yes. Yes, I will marry you."

The room erupted in laughter and hearty congratulations. When they turned and faced the crowed, Camille realized who the other customers were. They were nearly the whole Blakely Police Department, including the captain and his wife, and of course, Sawyer, and Esley.

Camille realized for the first time that she now had a whole new family. She would never be afraid again, never feel alone, and definitely never keep another secret. For the first time that she could remember, she felt free, and with that freedom came a love she never thought she'd have.

Tope kissed her again, and as the room died down, friends filed by one at a time, offering their congratulations and their love.

Chapter Twenty-Nine

Camille struggled with the fact that she'd not had any time to mourn her friend and protector, Tug Carlson. He was every bit the hero that the town knew him to be. She knew it even more than the town did.

In the weeks following the arrest of Henry Fitsimmons, Camille found more time to go through her father's things, stored in the attic of her new home. It was the first time she'd felt strong enough to explore the boxes, and to remember his life. She missed him so very much, and wished Tope had known him.

Tope wasn't able to help her bring the boxes down, which wasn't an issue for anyone but Tope. Camille knew full well she could bring the boxes down by herself, as she needed them.

In one of the larger boxes, she'd found her mother's journals and wept as she read personal information from her mother's time as a spy, a wife, and her short time as a new mother. Camille's feelings ran deep and the pain she felt at the loss cut into her heart, creating a longing she'd never felt…a longing to know the woman she would have called Mother. She was allowed to finally grieve for the mother she'd never had in her life, and grieve she did.

Pictures she'd never seen were made far more real to her through her mother's journals and pictures and also letters written between both her parents. The love her parents shared for each other, and for her, was real, and honest. Her father's grief at the loss of his wife was a pain from which he never could heal. He took great joy in his daughter, relishing in her successes, showing empathy and compassion in her failures. Camille felt the love of her father even stronger in these boxes of memories.

It was in one of the boxes that Camille found something that made her both proud of her heritage and stunned, at the same time. There was an entry in her mother's journal where she mentioned meeting a nice young man, a Marine Force Reconnaissance team member. He was strong and confident, as any Force Recon member would be, but she wrote on several occasions that there was something different about this Marine, something special.

Miriam Manning felt toward this young man as a mother would feel toward a son. She wanted to protect him, but he needed no protection. Somewhere in their friendship he became a confidante, someone she could tell things to that no one else, with the exception of her husband, would ever hear.

The young man's name was Tug Carlson. He was notoriously loyal and committed to his country, and to the preservation of it. It was for this reason she entrusted the same line of code hidden away in the file Camille found when going through Tug's files after his death.

In that same journal entry, her mother expressed concern for her new child, Camille. Miriam was fearful that if anything happened to her, the same fate might await Arthur, and where would her little girl be, with no mother and no father? She asked Tug if he would watch over her, protect her and keep her safe. Tug agreed to do that, assuring Miriam that nothing would happen to her little girl.

But, the one thing Miriam could never tell Tug, was that she would die protecting a group of operatives, a list of men and women that included his name. Because of his early death, Tug never knew Miriam's death was a sacrifice for him and for the others on that list. Miriam would go to her grave, protecting those brave souls, keeping the list from falling into the hands of anyone other than herself and her husband. She trusted *no one*, not even her own government, and because Tug's name was included in there, and she didn't even want him to know her secret.

When she gave him the line of code, Miriam told him only to guard the code with his life, and he did.

This last line, where her mother said he was *'to guard them with his life'* gave Camille great comfort. She was not the only reason Tug came to Blakely. He was to protect her from those seeking the documents, which he did, and protect the documents, as well.

In reading the journal entry, she understood clearer than ever before that Tug was doing his job as a Force Recon Marine. He was being a Marine. Tears fell from her eyes like water off a cliff.

Having moved back to the hotel a week previous, Tope arrived at Camille's home and knocked softly the front door. It was dinnertime and he had promised to take his beautiful bride-to-be to dinner and a movie. When she came to the door, he was surprised to see her so upset.

"What is it? What's wrong?" Tope sat down on the couch with Camille beside him and put his arm around her, holding her tightly. When she could speak, Camille raised her head from his chest and stared into his eyes.

"I want to do a memorial service for Tug Carlson."

"I believe he's already had a service, Camille, but we were so deep into the investigation we couldn't be there. I know Tug understands that."

"Yes, I know, but I need the world to know what I know about Tug, not the details of his life as a Marine, but that he came here to fulfill a promise to my mother, and he did that with his own life. I want people to know he died protecting me."

Camille explained to Tope what she had learned in the journals she'd found and he acknowledged her need to do this for Tug. Her request, though unorthodox, was easy to understand, and with Tug's standing in the community, it was not hard to convince the authorities of the need for the extra service. With permission granted, Camille and Tope set about planning a graveside memorial service.

There was an ad placed in the local paper announcing the day and time of the memorial. There were radio spots and interviews with Camille explaining what she wanted to do. The local news station also featured a story about the memorial, which allowed Camille to express her desire to talk about and thank her personal hero.

On the day of the service, a small podium was set up beside the grave for her to speak from. The service was open to the public, of course, but Camille wasn't sure how many, if indeed anyone, would come to hear what she had to say. She was stunned by the attendance of the townspeople, and very, very grateful.

There was a hymn sung, a prayer said, and Camille stood before a crowd of about fifteen hundred people, thankful for the PA system provided by the city for the event. As she began to speak, a hush blanketed the large assembly. Camille took a deep breath and began.

"I wanted to come here today to honor a good, kind man, Tug Carlson. I offer my humble and heartfelt thanks to him for what he did for me, and for the promise he kept to my mother. Tug, as you know, was a Force Recon Marine. He loved his country; he loved protecting all of us, as part of this great country. But what you didn't know is that he made a promise to my mother years ago. Because of the need to stay out of sight, my father changed our name and we moved to Blakely when I was just a toddler. Tug searched for me, and it took many years, but he found me. I'm afraid I will never know how. Tug died before I understood that he came to Blakely for me, and I am so thankful that he did find me.

"After my birth, my mother, aware that she was about to sacrifice her life for her country, asked a favor of this, at the time, young Marine. She knew that by not revealing her secret, she would die a traitor. For this reason, she is as much a hero to me as is Tug, for she died protecting operatives who were working to keep America safe.

"I believe Tug knew of her sacrifice to some degree. He honored her request, which was to watch over her daughter, to find and take care of me and protect not only me, but some very important documents he would find here.

"Tug somehow made himself my friend without divulging what he knew about my family. It didn't take long before I realized that I trusted him, and that felt very odd to me, but I knew it was true. And yes, he found those documents when he found me, and he protected them. When I told him people were threatening me he flew into action. He hired me as an administrative assistant so he could have me close to him each day, and he died three days later.

"Only recently was I made fully aware of all he did for me, and for many other people, as well. Tug, I thank you for your service, I thank you for your life. You are my hero. I am honored by your willingness to do what you were asked to do; I am honored to call you my friend.'

"Rest in peace, my most esteemed Marine. Rest in a peace hard fought. There are others who will take your place in your beloved Marine Corps, others who will fight as you did, who will give their lives for this country. And like you, they will answer the call of mothers all over America who pray daily for protection for their families. These men will take up arms and do what is required of them to fulfill their duty. But for you, my friend, your work here is finished. May the Lord take you in his arms and say to you, 'Well done my child. Well done.' God speed you home Tug and into His eternal rest."

After another song, the crowd slowly dispersed until eventually it was just Tope and Camille standing beside Tug's grave.

"That was beautiful, Camille." Tope gave her a gentle squeeze. "I know Tug must be so very proud of you."

"He deserves more than a memorial, Tope, so much more. He deserved the right to live his life and not be murdered. But sometimes, we just have to accept the hand we are dealt. I wish his hand had been a different one, but after all I've learned of him, I'm not sure he would agree with me." Camille paused and gazed up at Tope. "Now that I've said what's in my heart, I feel…lighter, somehow. I needed to tell him how I felt. Now I can move on, thankful for him and thankful for the life he helped save."

Tope nodded as the couple strolled slowly through the cemetery and out to their car. Life would move forward now, for both of them, just as it should.

Epilogue

It's said that traumatic experiences aren't great grounds for establishing a relationship. However, when it came to Tope and Camille, the things she'd learned about herself and her family only made her feelings for Tope stronger. She wanted a family that would never be torn apart by war and government agencies. She wanted a man she could trust with her everyday life, one who would be there for her when she needed some extra emotional help. She knew she'd found that in Tope. She knew it from the moment he'd stood beside her desk in Tug's office, checking on her, making sure she was okay.

When she'd told Tope she wasn't okay, he didn't even flinch. He was right there, and Camille knew he always would be.

The wedding turned out to be a lot bigger than Camille ever imagined. Police officers from the Blakely PD, all dressed in their uniforms, their wives and children beside them, attended the ceremony, which added to Camille's feelings of humble gratefulness for their kindness and friendship.

Her whole life had been lived alone. Never allowed friends to her house and never able to spend time at the homes of friends, she made no close associations and kept to herself. Though her father never explicitly told her it had to be that way, somehow, she always knew that was her only choice. Only now did she understand his paranoia when it came to their life together.

As she turned from the pastor to her husband, standing beside her, and faced a chapel full to overflowing with friends, did she fully understand the meaning of the word 'friend.' These were people who cared about her and cared about Tope. These same people would watch their family grow and be a part of every new experience in their lives.

Two weeks prior to their wedding, Tope received word that it would possibly be another year before it would be safe for him to return to D.C. The clean-up was taking longer than expected.

Tope spent many sleepless nights wondering if he should ask Camille if she would want to live in D.C. at the end of his 'exile.' How could he ask that of her? *He* didn't even want to live in D.C., and when he finally said that out loud, he understood why his path in life had wound through Blakely, Iowa.

When the newlyweds returned from their honeymoon, the first thing Tope did was call Cayman Richards and tell him he would be staying in Iowa, specifically Blakely, Iowa. Tope moved into Camille's home, had the remainder of his belongings shipped to Blakely and they began their lives together.

No more secrets. These became her three favorite words and were now painted on a plaque that hung over the front door of their home. That simple phrase had given her the freedom she didn't even know she'd longed for, until this whole situation burned the words into her heart.

Camille's favorite poem became another plaque in their home. It seemed her recent experience had made the words more real to her than they'd ever been before. It was Tug who'd taught her the lesson she now read in the words of that poem.

> Life is mainly froth and bubble.
> Two things stand like stone:
> Kindness in another's troubles.
> Courage in your own.

Adam Lindsay Gordon

THE END

Other books by JL Redington

Juvenile Series (8-13):

The Esme Chronicles:

A Cry Out of Time
Pirates of Shadowed Time
A View Through Time
A River In Time

Broken Heart Series:

The Lies That Save Us
Solitary Tears
Veiled Secrets
Softly She Leaves
Loves New Dawning

Passions in the Park:

Love Me Anyway
Cherish Me Always
Embrace Me Forever

Duty and Deception:
Novella Series

Erased
Entangled
Enlightened

Extracted
Eradicated

Come join me on
Facebook: Author JL Redington
Email: contact@jlredington.com
Twitter: @jlredington
Website: www.jlredington.com

Made in the USA
Charleston, SC
29 April 2016